Other books by Carolyn Brown:

The *Love's Valley Historical Romance* Series:

Choices
Absolution

The *Promised Land Romance* Series:

Willow
Velvet
Gypsy
Garnet
Augusta

The *Land Rush Romance* Series:

Emma's Folly
Violet's Wish
Maggie's Mistake
Just Grace

Love Is
A Falling Star
All the Way from Texas
The Yard Rose
The Ivy Tree
Lily's White Lace
That Way Again
The Wager

HB

D0857320

OFFICIALLY
WITHDRAWN

Brown, Carolyn, 1948-
Trouble in paradise.

HESPERIA BRANCH LIBRARY
9650 7th AVENUE
HESPERIA, CA 92345
760-244-4898

TROUBLE
IN PARADISE

TROUBLE
IN PARADISE

•

Carolyn Brown

**SAN BERNARDINO
COUNTY LIBRARY
SAN BERNARDINO, CA**

AVALON BOOKS
NEW YORK

© Copyright 2005 by Carolyn Brown
All rights reserved.
All the characters in this book are fictitious,
and any resemblance to actual persons,
living or dead, is purely coincidental.
Published by Thomas Bouregy & Co., Inc.
160 Madison Avenue, New York, NY 10016

Library of Congress Cataloging-in-Publication Data
Brown, Carolyn, 1948–
    Trouble in paradise / Carolyn Brown.
        p. cm.
    ISBN 0-8034-9744-X (acid-free paper)
    1. Women novelists—Fiction. 2. Divorced mothers—Fiction.
3. Mothers and daughters—Fiction. 4. Dwellings—
Remodeling—Fiction. 5. Home ownership—Fiction. 6. Texas—
Fiction. I. Title

    PS3552.R685275T76 2005
    813'.54—dc22

                                    2005021945

PRINTED IN THE UNITED STATES OF AMERICA
ON ACID-FREE PAPER
BY HADDON CRAFTSMEN, BLOOMSBURG, PENNSYLVANIA

With Love
to my friend,
Marlene Rucker

Dear Readers,

There really is a Spanish Fort, Texas right on the Red River where the Taovayas Indians settled back in the mid-1700s. The Chisholm Trail cattle drives really did go through there, and the oil boom in the '20s put almost as many oil wells in the area as there were Angus cattle. History says at one time there were four hotels, several saloons, several bordellos, and specialty shops in Spanish Fort.

There's not much left in the way of commerce in Spanish Fort these days, but there's a lot of friendly folk who live there, who'll wave at you when you drive through even though they don't know you. The old school built in 1924 still stands, a silent sentinel to more prosperous times.

To my knowledge, The Paradise was not the name of a single one of those bordellos . . . but it could have been.

Hope ya'll enjoy gettng to know Mary Jane, Joe Clay and the seven girls.

Merry Christmas,

Carolyn Brown

Chapter One

Mary Jane Marsh Simmons rapped lightly on the motel
door. Nothing. Not even a faint snore. Surely Joe Clay
hadn't already left. If he had she'd be in big trouble because
there didn't appear to be anyone else available to take care
of her problem. She knocked again; this time louder. Still
nothing.

"Joe Clay Carter, if you're in there, wake up," she yelled.
Two other doors opened. To her left an elderly woman, a few
strands of her lilac hair peeking out from the toilet paper
wrappings. To her right a girl with stovepipe black hair,
straight as a board, looking as if it had been cut with a dull
chainsaw, black eyebrows, eyelids, lipstick. Past and future
stood on either side of Mary but what she wanted was Joe
Clay Carter, present, to open the door.

"If you'll stop that hollerin', I'll wake him for you," goth-
girl said, peeping around to see the room number and then
going back into her room.

Instantly the phone in the room behind the door began to
ring, and ring, and ring. Finally, a muffled voice let Mary

1

know the man hadn't died in a Nocona, Texas motel in the middle of August. She pounded on the door again.

"Hold your horses," he bellowed. "Damn it! What did I do with my shirt?" The last spoken as loudly as the first.

The door swung open and Joe filled the empty space. Six feet four inches. Not a spare ounce of fat upon him. A scar running from his right temple down his cheek, giving his face even more character than the laugh lines around his crystal clear, bloodshot eyes. He wore a pair of skintight faded blue jeans and a t-shirt with the arms cut out. The small tattoo on his left upper arm sported a two inch knife with an insignia Mary didn't recognize emblazoned down the length of the blade. The tattoo had been added since high school. The rest looked the same, only a little older and worse for the wear.

"Can't you read, woman? The sign on the doorknob says 'Do not disturb'. Come back in an hour and I'll be gone. You can clean the room then," he growled.

"Joe Clay, open your drunk eyes," Mary said. "I'm Mary Jane Marsh. Remember me?"

"My eyes might be bloodshot, but they ain't drunk and what are you doing cleaning rooms in a Nocona, Texas motel? I thought you was some fancy big writer living the ritzy life down in Dallas," he leaned against the door frame. Yes, he remembered Mary Jane Marsh. How could he forget her?

Mary Jane was still a looker all right. She'd worn her black hair a lot longer in high school when she was head cheerleader and he'd been the quarterback on the football team. He could see a few wrinkles around her mouth, crow feet at the corners of her eyes. But hey, they were both thirty-eight years old. If there were wrinkles on their faces, they'd earned them. At least he had.

"And what does a big shot writer want with Joe Clay Carter this early in the morning?" He rubbed a fist across two days worth of stubble.

"A deal. I want to hire you. We'll talk over a cup of coffee up at the Dairy Queen. I'll give you fifteen minutes," she said.

"Hire me to what?" He didn't budge.

"Put on some shoes, Joe Clay, and meet me there in fifteen minutes," she turned to go back to her minivan, noticing the big black Dodge Ram sitting in front of his door. Great thunder, if he was driving something like that, he sure wasn't down and out on his luck and he could well afford to turn her down. She moaned, thinking about the repercussions.

"I'll meet you there, Mary Jane, but I'm not drunk and haven't been drunk," he said. "Not that it's one bit of your business after twenty years. You weren't a bit interested back then, so I'd suppose you aren't now."

"You got that right. And I'm glad you're not hungover, Joe Clay. Twenty years makes lots of changes so I didn't know if you were into the booze or not," she threw over her shoulder. "Fifteen minutes."

Joe watched her drive away in her shiny minivan. Was that the newest fad for romance writers? Did they carry their high-tech equipment in the back? A smile tickled the corners of his strong mouth. So Mary Jane Marsh had a job for him and she drove around in a bright red van instead of a little two-seater Porsche. Well, no one had ever accused her of following the crowd, now had they?

He pulled on his favorite scuffed cowboy boots and ran his fingers through his prematurely gray hair, turned that way in a single year back around the time the Gulf War had started. One day he had black hair; the next it was gray. Or so it seemed. Actually the process took about a year. Not that he minded. It, along with the scar, had sure put some good-looking women on his arm. *I should shave but why bother?* He asked himself. She hadn't been interested in old Joe Clay back in high school when she was just head cheerleader. Now that she was an important writer, it wouldn't matter if he had a two day beard or was shaven as smooth as a baby's hind end.

She'd barely started sipping her coffee when his big pick-up truck roared into a parking place right in front of the Dairy Queen. He swaggered up to the cash register and ordered a cup of coffee, not even looking her way. They'd had their petty teenage differences twenty years before, but she'd never liked Joe or his bigger–than–life–in–Texas ego. She didn't have to like him now; she just had to convince him to do the job.

"So who do you want killed?" He smiled lazily at her as he slid into the booth across the table from her. "I expect someone has told you some cock and bull story about how I was a mercenary or some such rot and now you think you can lay money on the table and I'll do a hit for you?" He chuckled.

"At the present time, I could think of one person," she grinned back. "But my sister is still an FBI agent in Houston and my brother is a Texas state highway patrolman. I expect neither of them would appreciate such a thing on their record. I can just see the headlines: "Woman Hires Hit Man." And the little sidebars would tease the reader with facts like sister of Federal Agent, sister of Highway Patrol, ex–wife of dead man."

"Divorced, are you?" He asked, stirring two heaping spoons of sugar into his coffee.

"Four years now," she nodded. "You?"

"Never married so I didn't have to become a national statistic," he sipped the coffee and added another spoon of sugar. "So what you got in mind, Mary Jane?"

"I moved back up here from Dallas. I bought the Paradise up in Spanish Fort. I want it remodeled. Been trying to find a handyman for two weeks. Finally, Geneva over at the City Hall called and said she'd heard you were back in town. She remembered your dad remodeling her folks' house when she was a little girl. Said you'd helped your dad that summer. I want to hire you to redo the Paradise," Mary told him.

"That old brothel? It's as old as God," Joe chuckled.

"Yes, it is. Built back when the cattle drives went through there. Back then it didn't have electricity or indoor plumbing, both of which need to be replaced and repaired these days. I had an engineer come up from Dallas. Said the foundation is solid as a rock and the house is good. But it looks like warmed over sin on Sunday morning," Mary said.

"What are you offering?" He let his eyes rove from her face down to her ample bosom.

"Not that, Joe Clay Carter," she said icily. "It wasn't up for grabs when we were kids and it isn't now. I'm offering a place for you to stay, room and board. It's got seven bedrooms upstairs and a nice big one downstairs. You can have the one on the ground floor. I'll make breakfast and supper. You're on your own for lunch since I spend my days writing. Six days a week until the job is finished with Sundays off. Probably at least until Christmas. I'll buy the supplies and you do the work. Name your price."

"Hmm," he was going to take the job and he'd do it cheap enough but be damned if Mary Jane was going to know that.

"Well?" She held her breath.

"I don't have to kill anyone and bury their carcass under the lilac bush?" He questioned.

"Honey, you'd be hard pressed to find a lilac bush on my property. Now if you'd be willing to bury someone under a blackberry thicket, that could be arranged. But I'm not asking for a killin'. Just a handyman to do or oversee a lot of work," she said.

"A thousand a week," he said.

"Five hundred," she argued. She could well afford a thousand a week, but Joe wasn't going to call all the shots.

"Eight hundred," he cocked his head over to one side. "And that's only if I like what I see when we get out there."

"Seven-fifty with a five thousand dollar bonus if it's finished by Christmas day," she shot back.

"Done," he held out his hand.

She shook it, only slightly amazed at how firm his handshake was, more puzzled by the sensation that his touch caused down deep in the pits of her stomach. "You need to go back to the motel?" She asked, her voice an octave lower, barely controlled. She sipped hot coffee in hopes he wouldn't notice.

"No, gave the woman my key on the way. Got my duffel bag in the truck. You ready to go?" He asked.

She nodded.

"Then lead the way. Who'd have thought my first job out of the military would be fixing up an old brothel," he muttered as he held the door open for her.

"I'd just as soon you didn't call it that. Just refer to it as Paradise," she said. "I'll lead the way."

"Whatever you say, boss," he opened the van door for her.

Seven miles north of Nocona, Prairie Valley School set over to the left. Kids were scattered over the playground. Joe Clay glanced that way but didn't let his thoughts tarry on all the children. He'd seen what the United States service could do to a marriage and a family. He didn't regret his decision to remain a bachelor, not even when he saw a little girl waving frantically from beside the swings.

Mary Jane waved at the child and noticed the sign out front welcoming everyone back to their first day. Maybe someday she'd write a book about this area. Instead of a Dallas heroine she'd have one from Nocona or Spanish Fort even. *Now wouldn't that be a hoot. Where would I find a hero in Spanish Fort, Texas?* The idea took hold as she drove and watched Joe Clay in the rear view mirror. *Could he be a model for my hero?*

She laughed aloud at such an idea. Joe Clay would think he was hero material if he was anything like he was in high school. But truth be told, he was too tall, too rugged looking, too real for an honest–to–goodness romance hero. As someone a lot wiser than Mary Jane once said, the truth is stranger than fiction.

Eight miles farther, one mile shy of going all the way into Spanish Fort, she slowed the van and made a left turn down a long lane lined on both sides with pecan trees. Five acres and a house, lots of pecan trees, a pond, detached garage, historical value. That's what the advertisement said. What it failed to say was the five acres hadn't seen a lawnmower in years and there were more weeds than grass. The pecan trees were covered in bag worms. The detached garage leaned slightly to the south. The pond was dried up with cracks big enough to hide an army tank inside. And how could an old brothel be written up as having historical value?

Mary Jane crawled out of her van and inhaled a double lung full of dust, boiling up from the tires of the big truck that Joe brought to a screeching halt in her front yard. She coughed and sputtered, waving the dust away from her face with her hands.

"Why on earth did you buy this old white elephant? Short

of the Baker Hotel in Mineral Wells, I can't think of another place on the face of the earth less likely to sell. But then I suppose writers have carved out the right to be eccentric," he leaned against the truck and looked up at the two-story house before him.

"I wanted the quiet and the room," she said simply. "The Baker Hotel still for sale, is it?"

"Last I heard and they're saying it would take fifty-five million at least to restore it," he grinned. "You remember going down there when we were seniors?"

"I remember," she smiled back at him. "Hadn't thought of that in years. Maybe I ought to do a paranormal romance about those ghosts."

"And I'll be the hero who saves the maiden in distress from jumping out the seventh story window," he chuckled. "Come on now, Mary Jane, this place is just as bad. Do you hear ghosts in the middle of the night here?"

"Haven't yet, but then one night can hardly hold the whole future, can it?" She said. "Come on inside. I want you to see it empty before the moving vans arrive. It will be easier to see what you need to do before the furniture is in place."

"Okay, but I'm telling you right now that Christmas will be pushing it, lady. To start with before we even go inside, the porch has some dry rot and the whole place needs to be scraped and painted," Joe eyed the outside carefully.

"Yes, we're painting it red," she said.

Joe Clay threw back his head and roared.

"Not brothel red," she almost blushed. "A deep red called red fox on the charts and trimmed with muted gold and antique white."

"Well, that can wait until later. What you probably want first is for me to sublet the plumbing out to a reputable company and get busy on the wiring," he stepped inside the front door behind her and back in time to when people built houses the way they wanted them instead of for convenience. The foyer was wide with a curving staircase off to the right. Joe remembered the place had been built for a brothel and could imagine the women in their satin and lace leading their customers up the stairs.

"I suppose the right place to start would be in the attic," Mary said. "That's where I saw a bunch of electrical stuff anyway. The air conditioning people are supposed to be here tomorrow to put in a couple of heat pumps. One for top and one for bottom," she looked back to make sure he followed her.

"They won't get them hooked up tomorrow Mary Jane. It'll take weeks to get the wiring done," he said.

"I want enough of it done by the end of this week so that we can begin using the central units," she told him, throwing open a door at the end of the wide hall. Steep, narrow steps led upwards into the attic. Stale, hot air hit them both in the face.

"What could you have been thinking, woman? Moving into an old derelict place like this in the middle of August. Only thing hotter than Texas in August is hell itself," he subconsciously drew his shoulders forward to climb the steps.

"It will be cool in a few days. Until then we can sweat," she brushed cobwebs from her bare arms.

"Well, it's solid enough, but this wiring is leftovers from the ark. It's a wonder the whole place hasn't gone up in flames," he touched the antique, cloth-covered wires. "My advice is to put in a brand new system. Leave the old in place. Put in a new air conditioning unit and then rewire each room as we do the work. I suppose that's what you had in mind. Refinishing the old girl, one room at a time?"

"I suppose," Mary's eyes wandered through the attic at the broken chairs and roll top steamer trunks under layers and layers of dust.

"So my first job will be to put in the beginnings of the new electrical wiring so you can write in comfort?" He asked, his eyes wandering up and down her figure. Tall. Twenty pounds heavier than high school. A few gray strands in her black hair along with cobwebs. Filled out her jeans entirely too well.

"Joe Clay, let's get one thing straight right now," she leaned forward into his gaze and stared into his baby blue eyes. "I wasn't interested in high school. I'm less interested now. A relationship, short or long-lived, isn't in my future. Don't mean to blow your sweet little bubble but all I want or need from you is good hard work. So stop looking at me like if you pushed me backwards, I'd fall on the floor and welcome you into my arms."

"Fair enough, but you can't blame a man for admiring the scenery," he blew her a kiss and followed the lead wire to the fuse box beside the attic window. Outside it connected up with a sweeping bundle of newer wiring that went straight to a pole out in the back yard. "I'll unload my things in this bedroom you're offering and go back into town. There's a lot of equipment at my dad's place that I'll bring out. That garage out there empty? I can work out of it, I suppose. How you want to do this with the supplies? Want me to keep the receipts and you reimburse me each week?"

"I suppose that would be the easiest, but do you have that kind of ready cash?" She asked.

"I'll manage," he said. She didn't need to know what his bank account looked like. "Now let's look at the upstairs bedrooms and bathrooms. What on earth could you be thinking about, buying a place like this? Just one woman to rattle around in it all day long. Such a waste of space. You could make do with a travel trailer. Hells bells, Mary Jane, you could live out of that minivan you got out there."

"I don't think so," she giggled as she made her way back down to the second floor. "Bathroom is right here. There are two of everything. Two toilets. Two tubs. No shower. I don't mind doubles. But I would like showers installed. The claw-foot tubs look to be in good shape and I love the idea of a soaking bubble bath in one of them, so maybe those wrap-around shower things you see in the old books. Brass, I think, would be nice. And take that closet out. Use the room for a long vanity with seven sinks and mirrors above them."

"Woman, you planning on running a hotel here? What would you need that many sinks for? Sounds like a bathroom in an airport," he wiped sweat from his brow. Maybe she wasn't so stupid after all, air conditioning this monster. At least he'd be working in cool air instead of heat that would make the Iraqi desert look like a snowstorm.

"I suppose it does. But it's what I want, so when you sub-let the plumbing, tell them that. Seven sinks. Pink ones. With a white countertop. Brass fittings," she told him. "Need to write that down?"

"I think I can remember something that crazy. Seven pink sinks. White countertops. Let's go look at the bedrooms, even though I won't get to them for a while," he said.

"Bedrooms are all basically the same. Seem to be the same size within a few inches," she led him back out into the hall and opened the door to the first one on their left.

"Big old rooms. You want to keep those high ceilings or drop them down to the normal eight feet?" He stared up at peeling wallpaper twelve feet up the walls and drooping from the ceiling.

"Keep them. I know it takes more to heat and cool the

rooms but while you've got the plaster and lathing off add insulation. That will help. And ceiling fans on those long extensions would be nice. Shiny brass," she said.

"Your call, boss lady," he drawled.

"Now I'll show you your room," she motioned him down the stairs. "I think it must have been where the original madam lived. It's bigger than the upstairs rooms and has an anteroom that was most likely her office. The anteroom also opens into the hallway so I've taken it for my office. You'll be working all day so I won't disturb you and when we redo the room I want the door connecting the two rooms covered up so it only opens from the hallway. I'll probably use your bedroom later, after you are finished with it, for a parlor."

"I'm sleeping on the floor?" He peered inside the empty room.

"No, you've got a king-sized bed, dresser, night stand, and desk on the way. Like I said, the movers will be here before lunch time. Any particular way you want it arranged?" she asked.

"Put the desk under that window so I can look outside while I work. The rest don't matter. I'm hungry. You said breakfast came with the job. I'd like four eggs, over easy, hash browns, sausage, a short stack of pancakes, and a pot of coffee," he said.

"Kitchen is this way. I can have that ready in ten minutes. You need a pencil and paper to make a list of the supplies you need for tomorrow?" She asked.

"You serious? You cook?" He asked incredulously.

"I cook. Breakfast and supper every day. Here's the notepad. You can sit at the kitchen table and make your list," she stepped through an archway into a big oversized country kitchen. The stove was so old the numbers were worn off the dials. The refrigerator rounded at the corners. The table, long and narrow, chipped in so many places it looked like it had been used for more than one butchering day, took up a good portion of the floor space. At least ten mismatched chairs surrounded it. Dirty dishes were piled on the counter beside the single, wall-hung sink with a hideous green and brown calico curtain stretched around the bottom.

"Kitchen is going to be a major remodeling job, but everything is functional for now. I paid extra to keep the table. There's a date on the bottom. Initials, too. CMR built it in 1864." She took eggs, onions, potatoes, and a can of biscuits from the refrigerator.

So she doesn't do dishes very often, he thought. At least she knew how to cook and the aroma of onions in hot grease sure smelled good. It had been weeks since he'd had anything but cafe food. When she'd promised two squares a day, he hadn't really thought she'd be doing the cooking. A double-sized electric skillet waited on the countertop. He watched, mesmerized as she poured pancake batter into perfect circles. He wondered why she'd never had children. He had no doubt that she would have made a good mother. What could her husband have been thinking about, leaving a setup like this?

Chapter Two

Joe Clay dreamed of machine gun fire, yelling soldiers, desert air so hot it tortured his lungs when he inhaled. He awoke with a start, sitting straight up in the king-sized bed, trying to get his bearings and remember where he was. The rat–a–tat–tat of the artillery were several pairs of feet going up and down the stairs. The yelling wasn't soldiers at all but voices out in the rest of the house. The window beside his bed was open and the warm air flowing across his bare chest promised another very hot Texas day, maybe not as hot as an Iraqi desert but not far behind.

He checked the clock beside his bed. Six-thirty. *What woman can get workmen out at this time of the morning?* He wondered as he shrugged on a clean t-shirt and wrinkled jeans from his duffel bag. This evening, after his work day, he'd unpack and arrange his things in the dresser. Checking his reflection, he ran his fingers through his silver hair and opened the door.

"Good morning," Mary Jane said from the doorway. She wore a pair of cutoff jean shorts, an oversized white shirt nearly as long as the shorts, and cheap rubber flip–flops on her feet. Her black hair was pulled up in a pony tail and she didn't have on a bit of makeup. "I just put breakfast on the table. You'll sit at the far end," she nodded toward the table. "I was about to knock on your door to wake you."

"Dreams woke me up. Who's in the house this early? You must have paid a fortune to get people to come out to work at the crack of dawn," he yawned and took his place, picking up the coffee pot and filling his cup.

"Breakfast!" Mary Jane yelled like a fishwife from the bottom of the stairs.

Joe Clay added two teaspoons of sugar to his coffee and waited. Evidently from all the food on the table, she'd gotten the men to come to work by offering them breakfast before they started their labor. Two platters of pancakes. Warmed syrup in one of those fancy little bottles like they use at Denny's Restaurant. A casserole that looked like it contained eggs, cheese, and sausage. Hot biscuits. Not from a can, either. From scratch. And a bowl of gravy. Joe Clay couldn't think of a single man in Montague County who'd pass up a chance at a breakfast like this.

From the sound of the feet on the steps, she'd hired every able-bodied man south of the Red River. For a fleeting moment he wondered if he should go ahead and get his plate filled so he wouldn't be left out. Food was the least of his worries, though, when what appeared to be half an orphanage giggled their way around each other to claim a chair. He counted. Seven of them. And all girls.

There were two things Joe Clay Carter didn't like. Kids were both of them. And girl kids were even worse than boy kids. They cried. They whined. They scared the bejesus out of him.

"Ursula, it's your turn to say grace," Mary Jane said as she took her place at the other end of the table.

Joe Clay opened one eye a slit to see which one would say the prayer. The biggest. Right next to Mary Jane. So that's why she bought this old brothel. She ran a school for girls and he'd promised with a handshake, as good as a binding contract in his world, that he'd be there until Christmas. Well, Joe Clay Carter had never broken his word in the thirty-eight years he'd lived, but that record was about to change.

"For this food we thank you, Father. And please help them get our air conditioning in real soon. Amen," Ursula said and the noise began. The very same sound of a military mess hall when the signal had been given for the men to begin their meal. Spoons clacking against plates. Words flying through the air like radio air waves. Only this was even worse. It was high-pitched girls' voices.

"Girls, this is Joe Clay Carter, the man who is going to make this house look like a mansion before Christmas," Mary Jane said.

All eyes were on him. Green eyes. Blue eyes. Even one set of light brown ones. Red hair. Brown hair. Two little blondes who were identical except for the tiny little scar under one's eye. Where on earth had she gathered up such a diverse group of girls?

"And these are my daughters," Mary Jane looked Joe right in the eyes without blinking, more than a little amusement hiding there.

"Do they all have the same daddy?" He blurted out before he even thought.

"No, we most certainly do not," the prayer-giving child answered just as bluntly. "My dad, and I am Ursula by the way, was a fun-loving student. He read me books and took me to the park while Momma worked."

"I'm Ophelia. My father was a beginning doctor. He worked long hours but when he had time, he wasn't too bad," the girl with kinky curly red hair sitting right beside Ursula told him.

"I'm Tertia. Third child and Tertia means third. My daddy was disappointed because I wasn't a boy. He told me he really wanted a son, but that I could be his boy since I was the last child. He took me fishing twice but most of the time he was much too busy at the hospital to spend much time with me," she said, stuffing her mouth with pancakes.

Joe Clay looked at Mary Jane, expecting her to tell them to hush and eat any moment. Surely she hadn't been married seven times.

"Our daddy was never around," the next little girl said. "I'm Bo and this is my twin sister, Rae. He said he had to make a living for an orphanage."

"And ours," the one sitting right beside Joe Clay looked up at him with the biggest, bluest eyes he'd ever seen. "Ours, mine and Luna's, we're twins too, was a sob. That's what Ursula says anyway. We're not sure what a sob is and she doesn't say it like that. She spells it out S.O.B . . . but we can read so we know what it spells. Anyway, our daddy divorced our mother when we were three and now he lives with Caitlin, who is richer than Midas in the book. I think he's a sob because he made Mommy let the nurse put a Q-tip in our mouths and send them off to check our DPA."

"Now that's our story," Ursula told him. "We each have a different daddy, but we do all have the same father. Even the DPA, as Endora calls the DNA test, proves that. And we see our father on Christmas, usually for a day before the holiday itself. Can you get me electricity in my room by tomorrow? I need an outlet to plug up my curling iron. Right now I'm having to unplug my CD player just to fix my hair and that's not so easy with the ceiling halfway to heaven and the only plug I've got in the whole room is the one on the side of the lightbulb socket."

"I think there's been a mistake, ladies," he wiped his mouth with the folded napkin beside his plate. "I found out that there was another job on my list and I have to do it before I can start this one." He pushed back from the table, his appetite gone, his nerves a bundle of raw wires attached to a run–run–run button.

"Chicken!" Mary Jane said behind her napkin as he passed her chair.

"So you're a sob too and you're going to leave just like my daddy did," Endora said from the other end of the table.

"You should teach her that that is not very nice. Even in the military we try to teach tact," Joe Clay said directly to Mary Jane.

"Teach them to tell the truth and then berate them for doing so? I don't think so. I didn't tell them all that. They figured it out on their own a long time ago," she said. "Never thought I'd see the day seven kids could scare the big, tough Joe Clay Carter."

"Well, you did," he told her, his blue eyes flashing pure electrical anger.

"A sob who runs off, just like my daddy," Endora said. "And me and Luna wanted some bookcases in our room so we can get our books out of the boxes."

Tension, thicker than gumbo, added to silence filling the room.

"I'll stay," he said, not believing that the words were out of his mouth. Surely some other fool had uttered them.

"Good!" Ursula said. "I'm the oldest. And I call rights to have my room done first."

"Is that fair, Mommy? And can we believe him? Does that mean he's not a sob?" Endora asked.

Joe Clay crossed his arms over his chest and waited.

"It's fair because Ursula is the oldest. But there's a possibility the bathroom will be done even before her bedroom and it will have seven sinks, all pink ones, with plug outlets and mirrors for each of you to primp to your heart's content. And yes, you can believe Mr. Carter. If he gives his word, he'll keep it. And he just said he'd stay, so I guess he isn't a sob after all, Endora. Now get your breakfast finished and brush your teeth. The bus will be out there in twenty minutes and right now there's only two sinks in the bathroom. And *you* can sit down and finish your breakfast. It's a long time until lunch or supper," she pointed at Joe Clay.

"I'm not Mr. Carter," he told the whole gaggle of girls. "You can call me Joe or Joe Clay. I'll refinish your rooms in the order of your birth. That's a fair way to do it. And all I ask is that you stay out of my way while I work," he went back to his chair and reloaded his plate with another round of food. Strange, it did taste much better with some of the heat gone from it.

Before he'd taken three bites, Ursula took her plate to the cabinet beside the sink, scrapped it clean into the trash can hiding behind the hideous curtains, and rinsed it. Tertia and Ophelia were next, followed by the older set of twins and then the younger ones. They all ran up the stairs to fight over the two sinks in the bathroom.

"Seven?" Joe Clay looked at Mary Jane quizzically.

"Seven. The first one was supposed to be a boy, Martin Joel Simmons the fifth. The second one was supposed to be a boy. We thought we'd try one more time. Tertia is number three, like she told you. That was it for us, no more kids.

Then there's that point five percent who get caught in the birth–control–didn't–work net and we had Rae and Bo. Marty had a vasectomy right after they were born. Declared he was tired of pink. Luna and Endora are the proof that he should have gone back to be sure the surgery worked. Wouldn't take a million bucks for any one of them; wouldn't give you a plug nickel for another one, though," she told him as she sipped her coffee.

"I can't imagine the child support," Joe chuckled.

"It would choke a good-sized elephant, but he's got it. I put him through med school and then he got mid-life crisis and married a woman who could buy a third world country out of her pettycash drawer. That's enough though. You don't need to see the dirty laundry on the line to put outlets in Ursula's room so we can sustain her vanity and my sanity," Mary Jane told him.

"You got that right," Joe said. "Good breakfast. I'm off to the attic while it's cool, if ninety degrees before the sun is barely up is cool. Mind if I make a gallon of iced tea to take up there with me? It'll save a lot of running back and forth and keep me from dropping dead with dehydration," he asked.

"Kitchen is open to whatever you want from now until sup-pertime. Lunch meat is in the fridge. Tea is in the canister marked as such. Sugar in the one beside it. There's a glass jug that pickles came in over there in the pantry. I use it every evening to make tea in for supper so please bring it back downstairs with you," she said. "And thanks, Joe, for staying."

"By the time the job is finished, you'll probably be glad to see this sob leaving," he said.

"I'm sure I will be. Most men either are or will be sobs. But we're two adults, not two teenagers, and we won't see each other all that much. I'll be up to my ears in deadlines and writing through the day while you're remodeling. Breakfast and supper. An hour at the most," she mused as she began the job of cleaning the table.

"Why didn't you like me in high school?" He asked as he set a saucepan of water on the burner to heat for tea.

"I could see through you, Joe Clay. You didn't fool me one bit. You were a sob back then," she laughed.

"So instead of going to the senior prom with a sob, you went out and married one," he shot over his left shoulder.

Instead of blushing, she giggled. "That I did. Sob or not, I'm not interested in a relationship, and besides, who'd want one with a woman who's got seven little girls with lots of years of raising left in them?"

"You sure got a point there. Me, I never cared much for kids. Lot of bother for nothing. Put your best years into them and what do you get for it? Heartaches and troubles," he said honestly.

"My girls have brought me nothing but happiness and joy," she bristled.

"Sure. That's because you let them call their father a sob without even correcting them. You should be telling them that he loves them even though he doesn't still love you. All that psychological crap that makes them grow up to be better women," he said.

"Tried that. Somehow actions speak louder than words, though. Conversation is over. Let's go to work," she said.

Suddenly, the stairs rumbled to life once again as the girls came running back down, shuffling through the pile of backpacks and lunch boxes on the floor.

"You didn't get mixed up and give Luna my lunch today, did you?" Endora looked at her mother, drawing her eyes down very seriously. "Yesterday I unzipped my box and there was a bologna sandwich. You know I don't eat any-thing that had a face, Mommy."

"First day mistake. Won't happen again. Don't fire me as your mother," Mary Jane kissed Endora on the forehead and sent her out the door.

Before the little girl shut the door she turned back, set all her things down, and reached up to Joe. "Pick me up, Joe Clay Carter," she demanded.

He did it, surprised at how light she was. No bigger than a bar of soap after a hard day's washing. "What is it you want to see from up here?" He asked.

"Nothing, I just wanted to see what it would be like to have a daddy hug me before I went to school. Now you can put me down. That's our bus coming down the lane," she said, matter–of–factly, wrapping her arms around him and hugging him tightly.

Both Mary Jane and Joe Clay were blushing and speech-less as she ran off to board the bus with her six sisters.

Chapter Three

In the still quiet of the early morning hours with only a lonesome whippoorwill singing his haunting melody of rejection, Rafael slid his muscular arm from under the body of the Lady Sephia lying next to him in the hay loft. They'd spent the night cuddled together, and now he had to go meet with the Prince, perhaps never to see his Lady again, never to feel her heart beat in unison with his, never to see her as anything but an English lady. An English lady who he had no right to since she was betrothed to the Prince, who would only be marrying her to please the King, his father. Oh, but once more, he'd awaken her with soft kisses on her eyelids. One more time he'd see those blue eyes go misty as he . . .

"Momma, where are you? We're home," Rae yelled from the front door.

Mary Jane rolled her chair back on the scuffed hardwood floor and stretched three hours' worth of tension from her neck and shoulders. Leaving her warrior about to kiss the heroine and the lady still asleep, she pushed the save button on the computer and quickly went to the front of the house.

23

Seven backpacks were thrown on the foyer table, seven girls in the kitchen cleaning out the remains of uneaten food and wrappers from their lunch boxes.

"So how did your day go?" She asked, leaning on the doorway, arms crossed under her bosom. Sweat trickled down the back of her neck and into every possible place it could find, especially the backs of her thighs where she'd been sitting for hours as she wrote.

"Hey," Joe said from the top of the staircase. "I think between me and the men you hired for the new air conditioning, we've got things ready to test. Don't look at the mess in the ceilings. We decided even though they're high, it would still be best to put the duct work in there rather than the floor. We'll use ceiling fans to blow more of the cool air around."

"Thank goodness," Ursula wiped her forehead with the back of her hand. "One more night of heat and I'll simply die."

"No, you wouldn't," Ophelia poked her in the arm. "Momma, is the Paradise an old ho–house? Richie said today in school that it was one. He said that it was built for a lady named Miz Raven who ran it way back in the western days when Spanish Fort was this big cattle town. He said his daddy told him you was crazy to buy it and raise little girls up in it. He said you was askin' for trouble. I can't believe Spanish Fort was a big town. Was it Momma?"

"What's a ho–house?" Endora asked.

"It's a place where you keep the hoes. Like the shed where you keep the shovel and the hoe and the dirt for the flower bed," Rae told her authoritatively. "Ophelia, you go on back to that school tomorrow and tell that Richie boy it's a real house, not a ho–house."

"What did you tell him?" Joe Clay bit his tongue to keep

from laughing. He didn't need anything in the kitchen but wild bulls couldn't have kept him at the top of the stairs where he couldn't hear Mary Jane's answer. She sure had her work cut out for her, raising up all those girls with all those questions. He was almighty glad at that moment that he hadn't married and didn't have a yard full of children.

Ophelia propped her hands on her hips, brushed her kinky red hair out of her face and rolled her eyes dramatically. "That I didn't know what it was built for way back then, but that we were remodeling it to be a house for nuns. And all seven of us had already been promised as the first ones," Ophelia said.

"Oh. My. Goodness." Ursula punctuated each word with a shake of her straight, dishwater-blonde hair. "So much for me ever finding a boyfriend now."

"What's a nun?" Endora asked. "Maybe I don't want to be a nun. What do I have to do to be one, anyway?"

"Want to explain that one?" Joe Clay asked Mary Jane.

"I thought I'd leave it to you since you've found so much humor in the whole thing," she said tersely.

"Not me. You had 'em. It's your job," he raised his hands. "But I'll tell you what ladies. Why don't we forget all about Richie and the Paradise and go upstairs to shut our doors and windows? I bet if we did that, we could test drive this new air conditioning unit we've been working on. Have to keep your doors shut tonight though, because it'll be tomorrow before we can get the downstairs unit in."

"Yippeee," Rae started the shouting and stampede up the steps.

"You side-stepped that one," Mary Jane followed him slowly up to the second floor. He filled out those jeans every bit as well as he'd done in high school, maybe even better. She could see muscles rippling under his sweaty, dirty shirt and something down deep inside her warmed.

"No, I didn't. I just diverted the troops long enough for you to reload your ammo and get ready for the next onslaught, General Mary Jane," he told her.

"That what you think of me?" She asked.

"Of course. It'd take a general to run a platoon like this," he looked back over his shoulder, his blue eyes twinkling.

Oh, no, she thought emphatically shaking her head, *this is not going to happen. He's not going to get past my armor with his smile or his tight-fitting jeans. Not now. Not tomorrow. Not ever. He doesn't like kids. I've got seven. Not even those tight-fitting wranglers and all those muscles can change that.*

Each bedroom had french doors that opened out onto a wide sleeping porch around the entire house. In its heyday, Mary Jane could envision women sitting out on the banistered sleeping porch in their satin finery watching the buggies and horses. So the people had already begun gossiping about her buying the place—and its history. *Let them talk*, she thought as she shut her own doors, blocking out a breeze that felt like it blasted from an oven. When she had the whole place remodeled, it would still be called the Paradise, but people would soon forget the past and think of it as the place where all those Simmons girls grew up. The one who was a rocket scientist, who came back home every Christmas. And that one who was a famous actress out in Hollywood who came back home every Christmas. Not to mention the one who set Nashville on its ear when she went there and who still comes home to sing at the church on Christmas. Or the one who won a Pulitzer for her work on *The Dallas Morning News* and literally put Spanish Fort back on the map. By the time Mary Jane had the doors shut, she'd rewritten the history of the Paradise so completely she felt like taking a bow.

"Air, blessed cold air!" Ursula exclaimed from inside her room. "Mom, can I do my homework in here instead of at the kitchen table? Don't open the door and let a single bit of this wonderful stuff out. Just yell through the door."

"Yes, you may. All of you go get your backpacks. Do your homework in your rooms and I'll sneak in each one to check it," she yelled.

"That a teenager's thank you I heard from behind the door?" Joe asked on his way back up to the attic.

"Barely. She just turned thirteen," Mary Jane told him.

"Good grief! Have you told the school officials she's only thirteen? She looks sixteen, tall as she is," he said.

"Have you been ogling my daughter?" Mary Jane challenged.

"I don't ogle young girls. I'm not that kind of man and you know it or you wouldn't have offered me room and board with the job, so stop insulting me. I'm just stating facts. She looks older than that. I've seen girls in the military that didn't look as old as she does. Besides if I'm of a mind to ogle, it would be with someone more my own age, and you've done laid down the rules where that's concerned. Not that you are my type either, sugar. I'm not interested in a woman who's richer than I am, who's got seven kids, and who shoots bullets from her eyes everytime she looks at me. If looks could kill, I'd already be dead," he all but growled back at her.

"I'll have to work on my aim," she retorted.

"Women!" Joe Clay slapped his thigh and went back up to the attic. He could work another two hours in the heat, maybe blistering some of the anger out of his soul.

"Men! Thank goodness all the babies I birthed were girls. I'd hate to think I'd contributed to the egotistical male population on the face of the earth," Mary Jane mumbled as she retreated back into her room. She picked up a pencil and a worn spiral-back notebook and flung herself down on the bed right under the vent in the ceiling. She'd take notes about the next chapter in *The Reckless Knight*. That's the way she wrote. A chapter at a time. No confining characters into a stiff outline, she let them breath and become real. She put the pen to the paper but no ink flowed.

"Okay, we've got about five minutes before lights out," Ophelia said from the middle of Ursula's bed.

"Are we in agreement?" Tertia asked.

"We'll take a vote," Ursula took charge. "All in favor of choosing Joe Clay Carter for our mission, raise your hand right now."

Seven hands went up in the air.

"Ophelia, what do you think? You're the smartest one of us," Ursula said.

"I think he's just fine. We agreed to leave Dallas because Momma needed someone, didn't we? Someone who wouldn't make her cry again like Daddy did. We're lucky to have found someone so quick. He's smart. He knows how to work. And he's even decided to stay until Christmas to fix this place up. That means we've got . . ." she counted on her fingertips ". . . four months."

"What's my job?" Tertia asked.

"To spy. That's what you do best. Keep your ears and eyes open and bring us the news every night," Ursula told her.

"Mine is to ask for help with my homework," Rae said. "I already started. When I heard him in the hall this evening, I took my book out there and asked him to check my multiplication."

Ursula giggled. "Girl, you've known those tables since you were four. I taught them to you."

"But Joe Clay don't know that, does he? I even missed a couple so he'd explain them to me," Rae giggled back.

"My job is to beg for a puppy or a kitten until he finds me one," Bo said.

"That's good, Bo," Ursula nodded.

"He doesn't like kids," Tertia blurted out.

"We know that," Ursula said. "That's the reason he left the table yesterday morning. He's one of those military men who was in the secret business. He hasn't had time to fall in love or have a family. We'll just have to help him see the error of his ways."

"How'd you find that out?" Ophelia whispered.

"There's a boy in my class that asked me if Joseph Clayton Carter was staying out here at the Paradise and did I know who he was?" Ursula said. "He said Joe Clay was one of those men like a Navy Seal. You know, like Steven Seagal. What he did was so secret he can't even talk about it. They've got it all sealed up in Washington, D.C."

"You mean he saved the world?" Luna's big blue eyes widened.

"Probably. And the bad thing is that I don't know if he's going to be able to make Momma like him. She knew him back in high school and she didn't like him then. And like I said, he doesn't like kids. We might ought to look around for someone else," Tertia said.

"But that was twenty years ago," Ursula said. "We'll just have to help them both."

"But he doesn't like kids, most of all girl kids. And it don't matter if he was an FBI agent or if he starred on "Law and Order" even. If he don't like kids, then we're doomed and we'll have to find someone else," Tertia said.

"Who?" Luna sighed. "Everyone we find, Momma turns down. Remember the dentist?"

They all nodded. Poor little Luna had put on quite a performance over an aching tooth so her mother would have to spend time with her dentist. Only to find out Mary Jane wasn't one bit interested in the man.

"We'll have to be more careful this time, is all," Ophelia said. "Endora, what's your job?"

"To hug him every morning. He might be big, but even big men like my hugs," Endora told them. "I like him. He makes Momma mad. Did you know there's not one word in her chapter book tonight? I checked it a while ago. There's always words in her chapter book at night. It's what she uses to type the next day. No one has ever made her not have her chapter book ready."

"Momma ain't never mad," Tertia said.

"Don't let Momma hear you say ain't," Ursula shook her finger under Tertia's nose. "Well, ladies, we'll give it our best shot. It's time Momma had someone to make her happy like Caitlin does Daddy. I think women get mad at the men they like. I sure do. First thing I usually do is get mad and then I decide to like the boy."

"You mad at anyone at school right now?" Ophelia asked.

"No, not yet," Ursula said.

"I'd like a daddy who's here all the time rather than one who's only here one night and day at Christmas," Luna said wistfully.

"Okay girls," Mary Jane knocked on the door. "Gossip time is finished. It's bedtime. Nine o'clock."

"Yes, Momma," seven voices said in unison as they high-fived each other and all but Ursula paraded out into the hallway.

The night air was stifling hot. Not a cloud in sight and no rain predicted for the whole week. Joe Clay kept a steady rhythm going with the toe of his cowboy boot in the old porch swing. The chains were rusty and rivaled the crickets' soliloquy in their high-pitched squeak. Tomorrow he'd apply a little oil to the eye bolts that held the whole apparatus in the porch ceiling.

Two days and the air conditioning units hummed, piping in cool air for the future nuns who lived in a former brothel. He grinned and slapped at a mosquito trying to feast upon his cheek. He couldn't see that one who'd needed help with her homework in a nun's habit. She was a pretty smart little girl. Or that one who demanded hugs from him as well as her mother before she went to school the past couple of days, either. They seemed to be pretty good kids, for a bunch of girls.

So far it hadn't been so difficult. He'd kept busy all day. Then after supper he'd gone to his room and made a list of what he would do the next day. Routine. Breakfast with the troops. Send them off to class. Work all day. Supper with the troops and go to his office for the evening. Other than that one hug he couldn't get out of and helping one of those twins with her math, he hadn't fraternized with the troops. Christmas would be here before he knew it. They even had a set bedtime according to what he had heard Mary Jane tell them at the supper table. Nine o'clock. That cleared the coast for a while on the porch swing if he wanted to get out of his room.

"Ah, I see you've laid claim to the swing," she said from the doorway.

"Room enough for two," he scooted over. "Promise I won't even try to lay my sweaty arm on your shoulders."

"It's too hot for cuddling, even if it wasn't Joe and Mary." She timed it just right so the swing didn't wobble.

"That's the truth. What do you mean by that? And while

we're at it, why did you turn me down that one time I got enough nerve to ask you out?" He asked.

"There never was a future in the Joe and Mary story. You just asked me to go to the prom because your girlfriend broke up with you. I wasn't going to be a stand-in," she said.

"Nice to have that cleared up after all these years. I figured it was because I had a scar on my face or bad breath," Joe said.

"Oh, hush, you did not," she started to slap at his arm but refrained. That could be misconstrued as flirting.

"Got the troops to bed, did you?" He changed the subject.

"Just now. I try to give them five or ten minutes of gossip time before I play the . . . what was it you called me . . . the major?"

"The general," he grinned. "What is gossip time?"

"Time for them to say they're sorry if they hurt someone's feelings. To vent if they've got a problem. To be friends," she said.

"Good concept. What did they talk about tonight?" He asked.

"Oh, it's their time. They don't think I know about it and I never butt in. I'm sure tonight's topic was whether Ursula is ever going to be allowed to wear makeup, which she can when she is fifteen. Whether Bo is ever going to get a puppy or a kitten, which I'll think about. Whether the Paradise was ever a brothel, which I'll explain later," she laughed.

"Just girl stuff then. That's what they talk about?" He yawned.

"That's it. After all, they're seven, eight, nine, eleven, and thirteen. What else would they talk about?"

Chapter Four

Mary sat in front of a blank computer screen. For the first time in eleven years there were no words. Nothing. Nada. Nil. She'd heard of writer's block and spelled it L-A-Z-Y, all capital letters. She'd even presented workshops on it, not understanding for a minute how anyone could ever run out of words.

She felt a presence rather than heard the slight knock on the door frame into her messy office. When she jerked her head around, Joe Clay filled the doorway. "What?" She snapped.

"Well, who poured vinegar on your pancakes this morning?" He raised a dark eyebrow. "If you can tear yourself away from that computer for a minute, I've got a few questions. Then I promise not to interfere with the romance queen of the South."

"Why did you call me that?" she asked.

"Read it in a review one time. I've got something I want you to approve in my room. Do we have to go around the hallway or is it all right to open that door?" he asked.

She slung open the door, surprised to find his bed made without a wrinkle, everything in the room military straight. "What is it?"

"Over here," he pointed to the desk under the window. "I need to talk to Ursula, or is it Ophelia? The oldest one of the bunch. But I wanted your approval first. Didn't want to start a war between you and your daughter."

"It's Ursula," she said shortly.

"Why'd you give them such weird names? Why not something easy like Mary or Jane or Sue?" He unrolled a long tub of paper and set four rocks on the corners.

"I wanted my girls to have something unique in their names. Something uncommon," she said. "When Ursula was born I was writing my first novel. The heroine's name was Ursula. I wanted to give all the sass and brass in that character to my daughter. She was never to be needy or clingy when she got older."

"All of them named for women in your books?" He smoothed the paper.

She nodded. "Every one of them. Ophelia was a woman in a castle romance. Tertia was the third daughter in a trilogy set in Ireland. Rae and Bo were women in a contemporary set in Louisiana. Rae was the police chief. Bo was the singer. Luna was a goddess in a book set right after the fall of Troy. And Endora, well, she was a blonde-haired vixen witch. What is this?"

"I can sure enough believe that about Endora. That's the blue prints for Ursula's new room. These are the doors out onto the upstairs porch. This is the door into her room. The other two walls are unbroken. There's sixteen feet on either, but the doorway in from the hall isn't centered so the closet needs to be on this other wall. I figured I'd give her twelve feet of closet space, then use the other four feet for built-in shelving. And rather than put the closet all the way to the ceiling, I'd set it in with open shelving up above it. The four feet beside the closet could house her books, and the upper part, since it's too high for books, could hold her treasures. I plan on buying pre–made bi–fold doors. They hold up better than sliding doors. She can decide on the colors when I get to that point. Only thing is when I build this, there's liable to be six others wanting about the same thing and I didn't know if you wanted to be out that much money," he said.

If pen strokes were words, Joe Clay hadn't been struck with writer's block. Even she could see the magnificent job he'd done. "When did you take architecture?" She asked.

"Didn't. Got my training in drafting. Not a whole degree but enough to be able to do this kind of work. Figured when I retired, I'd need something to fall back on. What do you think?" He asked.

"It's wonderful. And I can afford anything you want to build, Joe Clay. I sold the house in Dallas and really need to put as much of the profit into this one to keep from having to give it all to the tax man," she said. "I like the idea of open shelving. They've got so much old stuff it's unreal. That extra bedroom upstairs is full from top to bottom with boxes of their things I won't let them unpack."

"Then I'll show it to her tonight and get her approval," he said. "And there's another thing we need to discuss. If you really want everything completed by Christmas, I need to hire in some help with the outside. I talked to the shop teacher at the school. He's got a few boys who'd be willing to work on Saturdays to scrape and paint the outside. I'll do the carpenter work, boards needing replaced, and such things as that. I called a company about putting in new windows. They'll be here tomorrow to give you an estimate. Got these new ones that look just like the old antique ones, sash and all. But that'll be your decision. I figure the boys can begin scraping even when the window men are working. Saturdays we can devote to outside work. If we don't get on it, cold weather will set in and you can't paint in cold weather."

"You'll supervise the whole thing? Saturdays are my shopping days. The girls and I normally buy groceries and spend the day doing something together. Sundays are for church," she explained.

Joe Clay could have kissed her on the spot. He'd worried about seven girls being underfoot on Saturdays. "Of course, I'll supervise. They'll think they've joined the military before the job is finished. It'll take at least two Saturdays to get ready for paint, but you need to decide what color this old girl is going to be."

"I told you before. It's called red fox," she said.

"You were serious!"

"Serious as child support on seven kids," she nodded.

"You're asking for trouble. Painting it a brothel red," he shook his head.

"It's a deep country red. The trim is called muted gold. And at that it's toned down from what Endora wanted. She thought a bright pink would be nice, with baby blue trim and white lace curtains in all the windows," Mary said.

Joe Clay's nose snarled in spite of his attempt to keep a straight face. "You'd expect that from a child. But a woman should know better than to paint a house red. I sure wouldn't want to live in a red house."

"Then red it certainly will be," she snapped and went back to her office, slamming the door between the rooms emphatically.

She slouched down into her chair, the blank monitor screen all but screaming defeat. She pushed the button to start whatever CD had been left in the machine beside the computer. Toby Keith began singing about how he should have been a cowboy. She thought of Joe Clay in the next room. He'd have her paint the house a pristine white if he had his way. Just like the cowboys who'd brought cattle up the Chisholm trail. Those who visited the Paradise in its heyday. She laid her hands on the keys and the words began to dance across the screen. Toby sang about a man who wasn't worth missing. A smile twitched at the corners of her mouth when Toby said that love was a good thing.

Yes, it was a good thing when it brought her reckless knight and his lady into the same room. It was good when her readers found escape in the pages. But was love really a good thing? She typed a scene where the knight begged the lady to give up her position and run away with him. Surprised that she'd finished ten pages, Mary leaned back and reread what she'd written.

"Love is a good thing," she snapped at the screen when she'd made a few corrections. "Then why am I raising seven little girls all alone? If it was such a good thing, why is Martin running around all over the world with Miss Bimbo Queen?"

She picked up a thick mug of cold coffee and downed the bitter contents. History couldn't be rewritten and if she hadn't had those years with Martin, she wouldn't have her girls. On the balance scale, she was still ahead. She laid her fingers on the keyboard and there were no words. She sat through three Toby Keith songs and waited. She reread what she'd produced. Not good. Not bad though. At least the day hadn't been a total bust. Maybe all she needed was a cup of hot coffee to jump start her again. What was it she told her audience about writer's block? Go walk a mile on the treadmill or around the house four times. Take a long soaking bath. Relax the mind. Make it empty. Then think about the heroine and what she'd like to be doing right at that moment.

A long soaking bath was out of the question. The plumbers were reworking the upstairs bathroom. The downstairs one had only a walk-in shower. Relaxing the mind was easier said than done. She worried that writer's block would be permanent. Think about the heroine and what she'd like . . . she'd like to run away with the knight and tell the prince to kiss her fanny. But that wasn't in the cards; not yet, anyway.

Mary Jane wandered up the stairs. Peeked in on the plumbers in the upstairs bathroom. They'd jerked everything out except the bathtubs and were running new pipes in from outside that day. The small downstairs bathroom had had to accommodate all seven girls before they went to school. Joe Clay had hired two separate plumbing companies to work hand in glove to get the work done quicker, but even at that, they'd said it would be at least a week. Every one of the old pipes were being replaced with the newer plastic, and then there would be a new septic tank installed.

"You lookin' for Joe Clay? He's over in that bedroom," one of the plumbers looked up from under the long vanity that would hold seven sinks.

Then she sure wouldn't go into the bedroom, but she didn't tell him that. She opened the door to the attic, amazed that a blast of cold wind hit her in the face rather than hot, musky air. So Joe Clay had thought to have the attic air conditioned. Well, bless his little heart. She carefully shut the door and went up to see what other changes had been made.

Insulation filled the spaces between the studs and there was a duct in the floor shooting cold air up into the odd-shaped room. She could see where Joe Clay's arms had dusted the area around the duct work and where he'd brushed against the roll top trunks as he moved them out of his way. She reached for a wooden kitchen chair with a broken back and sat down next to the attic window. She threw the lid of an old trunk back, expecting to find disintegrated lace curtains, but it was full of books. She picked one up and opened it carefully.

Today I hung the sign above the archway out on the road. Now I guess there's no turning back. The Paradise is officially open for business. I've recruited seven girls. Eight of us and we'll be rich before the end of this era. Where there's money, there's men willing to spend it. And they'll pay for quality. We'll give them that and the Paradise will be known for its high class. The other places might get more business but we'll have more money because men do like their little luxuries. If I learned nothing else from my mistake with the Duke, it was that. So everything stands ready. Come to the Paradise and leave a new man.

Miss Raven

A loud boom shook the floor under Mary's chair. She put the book back into the trunk but didn't shut the lid and hurried down the stairs. Lawsuits flashed in front of her eyes. A plumber had fallen through the ceiling and broken his neck. Had Joe Clay thought about workman's insurance?

Another loud boom shook the house by the time she reached the hallway. Good grief, were they all falling to their deaths? She checked the bathroom where the plumbers were still working. The floor was intact. No one was screaming for an ambulance.

The third boom rocked the souls of her bare feet. "What is going on?" She yelled.

The door to Ursula's bedroom flew open. "What are you doing up here? You're supposed to be down there in your little messy office, writing stories for bored housewives," Joe Clay stood there with a sledge hammer in his hands.

"My office is not messy and I'll have you to know not all women who read romance novels are bored housewives. Sometimes even men read my novels," she propped her hands on her hips. "What are you trying to do? Tear down my house or make it fall around me in a heap?"

"I'm knocking three or four holes in the wall so I can have a place to begin. The plaster and lathing has to come off so I can insulate and sheet rock," he shot right back at her. She had dust all over her white t-shirt and shorts. Her chin sported a dime-sized clump of dirt with a cobweb hanging from it. But somehow she sure didn't look like the wicked witch of the West like her stance portrayed. "You do want this place done by Christmas, don't you?"

"Yes, I do. My whole family is coming to spend Christmas day with me and I want it finished by then," she said.

"Then I'll get back to work," he left her standing in the hall.

She wished she could jerk that big oversized hammer from his hands and hit him a few times with it. Anything to work out the frustration of having acute writer's block. No it wasn't his fault she couldn't write that morning, but he could be her scape goat. Not knowing what else to do, she went back to her computer. She looked at what she'd written and tried to make herself write. Nothing happened. She pulled up a blank screen to use for brainstorming.

"A woman's touch is what men need. Not just the physical act of making love, but all the little things that go into making him feel special. A tender hand to smooth the rough and ragged edges. To make him leave this place thinking he'd just visited heaven and took a piece of Paradise with him," the madam said as she began to train the seven girls she'd recruited from a brothel in New Orleans.

"Good lord," Mary Jane exclaimed as she drew back and looked at the words she'd written. She backed up and titled the work. *The Madam of Paradise*. And began to write, words describing the first night the Paradise opened for business. The sound of the sign squeaking as it swung back and forth in the hot summer breeze. The smell of hot, fresh bread wafting out the kitchen window as the cook prepared food for the customers. The scented soap sitting ready for long, soaking baths. She didn't hear the plumbers laughing and talking as they worked or Joe Clay ripping the walls out of Ursula's room. More inspired than she'd been since the first book she'd written, she filled page after page with the story of Raven and her first night of business, when the big, black butler named Jems only let eight men through the gate and past the sign before he slapped on the lock.

At noon, Joe Clay stopped by her door on his way to the kitchen to make himself a sandwich. She was so intense he didn't even knock. He took his lunch to the front porch and ate it on the swing. Not that they'd ever shared their mid-day meal anyway. Usually he made his food and took it outside for a breath of fresh air, even if it was hot as blue blazes. At least it got him outside for a few minutes.

Mary kept writing until her growling stomach insisted she stop. When she looked at the clock it was well past two. The girls would be home in an hour and a half and she hadn't even thought about after school snacks or supper. She proofed her inspirational outburst and wrote a short note to her editor, attaching the first two chapters of the book. She told Norm, her editor, that she'd had a sudden brainstorm. That she'd definitely meet the deadlines on *The Reckless Knight*, but that she wanted him to take a look at this and render his opinion. She pushed the send button and went to the kitchen where she nibbled on an apple and made a fruit

tray with some of Rae's favorite dip. The kind where she
added frozen strawberries to a marshmallow cream and
cream cheese mixture. The girls would love that for an after
school snack, even if it wasn't more healthy than cookies
when she considered the dip. She decided to make spaghetti and meatballs for supper and gathered the ingredients
from the pantry. She picked up the big metal bowl she mixed
yeast bread in on her way back out and mixed a raising of
bread. Spaghetti, hot fresh bread, and a big salad.

She finished the apple and made herself a peanut butter
and marshmallow cream sandwich. That brought back memories of when she was a child and carried the same lunch in
her lunch pail to school. Only once did she let her best
friend, Betsy, talk her into trading. She hadn't thought about
Betsy in years. Last time they had a class reunion Betsy
couldn't come. Jim, her husband, had just been transferred
to Newport News, Virginia. Mary made a mental note to call
Betsy's mother and ask about her.

She filled a tall glass with milk and wandered back to her
office. Maybe she'd try to work a while longer on her knight
story. She had at least an hour before the girls came dashing
through the door, bringing enough energy and noise to keep
Mary from being able to think about a story line.

Mail. Mail. Mail. A little message flashed across her
screen. Ursula had set it up to do that when there was email.
It's probably something from mom, she thought as she pulled
up the message.

She laid the sandwich aside and wiped her mouth with the
back of her hand. Gulped down half the glass of milk. It was
from Norm and marked urgent. Even after more than a decade of writing, she still got clammy hands when she sent in
a proposal. He'd tell her to stop meandering around with
some crazy story of a brothel, of the mistress of it falling in

love with the local sheriff, of all that folderol about men wanting more than a romp in the hay. She swallowed the golf ball-sized lump in her throat and got ready for a rejection and a lecture about staying focused on her knight story.

She shut her eyes and clicked twice. When she opened them, she read:

STOP the knight story. You are well ahead of deadline and you can finish it after you get this one done. Go with this. It's flowing from the heart and reads like your first work, full of descriptions that give me the chills it's so good. I can already see a big white house on the cover. With a porch upstairs that wraps around the whole house, and a sign above the entrance into the property. Don't stop. I want what you do sent everyday. Can it be done by Christmas?

Norm

Chills chased up and down Mary Jane's spine as she read and reread his note. But white? White! Surely she could talk him into a red house on the cover. Red for an old brothel. *No,* she argued with herself. The Paradise would have been white, even in the beginning. There was nothing about the old brothel that said it was cheap and housed a bunch of floozies. Miss Raven was a lady of the first degree and she wouldn't have had a red house or even red drapes hanging in the bedrooms. They would have been airy and feminine with flowing lines, to make a man leave feeling like he'd truly visited heaven.

She picked up her chapter book and went back upstairs to the attic. She'd take several of the journals to her bedroom and fill her book with notes.

"Hey, come and see what I found!" Joe Clay called from the bedroom when he saw her pass by the door.

"What?" She stopped outside the door. He'd torn a complete wall down, leaving only the studs showing. By the end of the week, he'd be ready to start hanging sheet rock.

"I guess it filtered down through the attic back before they put the floor up there. It's an old tin type. I think it's this place back when it was first built. There's a bunch of women on the porch. Look at them, Mary Jane. They don't look one thing like you'd think women like that would," he handed her the picture.

Eight women stood on the porch of the house and it was indeed white as the clouds of heaven. They were dressed in white flowing robes that covered every inch of their skin. High necklines of lace. Their hair dressed high on their heads in the fashion of the day. Smiles on their faces. They looked more like Sunday school teachers or pure angels than they did fallen women. But then, that's what would make the men give up their hard-earned dollars, wasn't it? A night in Paradise.

"I've changed my mind about the color, and I don't want to hear a word of 'I told you so' from you because you have nothing to do with the decision. I want it to be the purest white you can find in a paint can, Joe Clay. All of it. No separate trim color," she said.

"Well, what brought that on?" He asked. "That old picture?"

"Doesn't matter what brought it on. It's the way it needs to be. I'll take this to a professional frame shop and have it matted and framed. It's going to hang in my office," she said. "Thanks for giving it to me."

"Hey, boss lady, it's yours. It's your house anyway. I just found it. Could be there's more up there in those old trunks. Who knows what we'll find in the rest of these walls," he said.

"I'm not major or general or even boss lady, Joe Clay,"

she said, her feathers more than a little ruffled. "I'm just Mary Jane."

"Yes, ma'am," he saluted smartly. "And just for the record, I think the place will be beautiful in white. Whoever painted it this horrid shade of turtle–dung green should be put to death by torture."

"At least most of it is peeling off. When we came up here to look at the place, the first thing Ursula said was that it would look better hot pink than the color it is now, but she wanted it white. She got outvoted by her mother," Mary Jane said.

"Smart girl," Joe Clay went back to work with his wrecker bar, adding to the enormous pile of rubble in the middle of the bedroom floor. He might decide to like that girl if she had that much sense at only thirteen.

A few minutes before four the front door opened and a rush of giggles stormed inside the house. Ursula dropped her books on the floor and ran upstairs to check the progress in her room. She hadn't liked the idea of moving her bed and bare necessities into Ophelia's room, but when her room was finished she could unpack all her belongings and really make a nest.

"Oh, no!" She put one hand over her mouth and one over her eyes. "I'm going to be old and gray before it's finished!"

"No, you won't," Joe Clay barked. *Give me patience*, he prayed silently. *Girls! I knew they were worse than boys.* "I thought you'd be pleased with the results. Look, I got two whole walls torn out already."

"I thought you'd have it nearly ready for me to move back into," Ursula sat down in the doorway, unblinking, hardly able to believe the mess that was to be her haven of privacy.

"Well, you thought wrong. I'll be another day tearing it away. One past that to get the insulation in. Another two or three to get the sheet rock up since the ceilings are high. Throw in another one at least for bedding and taping and then I can start the closets and finish work," he told her. "But after supper I've got the plans drawn up for you to look at. Your mother has already okayed the expense if you say they are suitable for you."

"You mean I get a say–so in what you're going to do with it?" Ursula brightened. "I suppose I can endure Ophelia's constant chatter a little while longer if I get to make some of the decisions."

"Two weeks?" he asked.

"Of course," she swallowed hard. He'd never have this room ready in two weeks. Not even if he hired a whole army of men. He might be able to save the world, but he couldn't do the impossible.

"Then I'll get back to work," he said, ignoring her as she sat there and watched him.

Joe Clay was the last one to the supper table that night. He took his place at the end of the table, Endora on his right, Luna on his left. Ophelia gave thanks and the noise began. Richie had said that they couldn't go to his church in Spanish Fort if they were training up to be Catholic nuns. Ophelia had told him that they could go anywhere they wanted. That maybe they weren't being brought up to be Catholic nuns but Baptist nuns.

"And what did he say to that?" Joe Clay asked.

"He said there wasn't any such thing," Ophelia slathered real butter on her yeast roll. "So I told him, of course there wasn't. We would be the very first ones in the whole world."

"I still don't know if I want to be a nun. Somebody has to tell me what it is, first," Endora said.

"It's a woman who gives herself to the Lord forever. She wears a black dress and a black thing on her head and she don't ever get married to a good looking man or even an ugly one," Luna said. "Remember what Whoopie Goldberg wore in that movie where she was playing like she was a nun? They call them sisters or mother."

"Well, I ain't bein' one of them," Endora said. "So you can just go on back to the school and tell that Richie guy that one of the sisters ain't going to be a nun."

"Isn't," Mary Jane corrected her grammar.

"That too. I ain't and I isn't. So there," Endora said. "Daddy, I mean Joe Clay, would you pass the salad dressing? The white kind. I don't like the red."

Joe Clay blushed as scarlet as the french dressing. He cleared his throat and kept his eyes on his plate.

Mary Jane's eyes snapped up at her daughter who was busy covering her salad with ranch dressing. She didn't act as if she'd just made the blunder of the season but then she was only seven and probably couldn't even remember when her own father had sat at supper with them. She'd only been three when the divorce was final. Martin had moved out more than a year before that.

"Nice move on the daddy thing," Ursula told Endora that night when they had their ten minutes of gossip time.

"It sure made Momma forget about the isn't and ain't thing, didn't it?" Endora said, wincing when Ophelia hit a snag in her long blonde curls.

"Sorry about that, kid," Ophelia worked the tangle out with her fingers before she began brushing again. "There's a rat's nest back here."

"So have you found anything, heard anything?" Ursula asked Tertia.

"Momma's working on a new story and she's got these old books in her room. Joe Clay was whistling and I heard him talking on the phone to someone, telling them to send the help on Saturday and that Mary Jane had decided to paint the whole place white after all," she said.

"She wanted red. I wonder how he talked her into white," Ursula cocked her head over to one side.

"Think she might be liking him? Maybe he likes white and she's doing it for him," Rae said.

"I don't think so. He's out there on the swing and she's in her room working on her chapter book. I'll sneak out on the balcony after she tells us to go to bed and see if she sits on the swing with him. She only did it that one night and I couldn't hardly hear what they were saying because the swing was so loud," Tertia said.

"You keep spying. And you're doing a wonderful job, Endora. Have you started on the puppy idea?" Ursula asked Bo.

"That's the Sunday job," Bo said. "After church when no one is busy. I'll ask Joe Clay if he could find me a puppy and then Momma will say I can't have one. That will make them talk to each other."

"Okay, girls, time for bed," Mary Jane yelled from the hallway.

They high-fived each other and ran outside to kiss their mother goodnight.

Joe Clay kept a steady rhythm with the toe of his boot as he thought about Endora innocently calling him daddy. The word hung like a brick on a thread above his head. It scared the devil out of him. It had only been the slip of a child's tongue, for sure. After all, he'd been sitting at the head of the table where the man of the house would be if he was the father. And she'd been riled up about being a Baptist nun. A chuckle erupted when he replayed the supper scene about

Baptist nuns. So she'd already been talking and that word just slipped out—*daddy*.

He wished Mary Jane would join him on the swing again, but evidently she was fighting a deadline because after she'd told the girls it was bedtime she disappeared back into her room. Tomorrow was Saturday and the paint crew would arrive at eight o'clock. That would keep him busy all day and the next day was Sunday. He'd already made plans to go to Wichita Falls on Saturday night and visit an old friend. Play poker all night and sleep in a hotel room all day Sunday. By then he'd forget all about some little blonde haired girl calling him daddy. Or wishing that the little girl's mother would join him on the swing either.

Chapter Five

Mary Jane put the finishing touches on Sunday break-fast. Waffles with melted butter and syrup or fresh straw-berries and whipped cream. Sausage patties and bacon for everyone but Endora who decided a year ago she didn't eat anything that had a face. Peanut butter and honey for her waffles.

"Can I go wake up Joe Clay now, Momma? Please?" Endora danced around in her bare feet, blonde curls still tangled from sleep.

"Just knock on his door and ask him if he's planning on going to church with us," Mary Jane said.

Rae, Bo, Luna, and Endora all took off down the hall like a herd of elephants.

"Hey, I told Endora she could wake him, not the whole bunch of you," Mary Jane called out. In only a week, Endora had adopted Joe Clay as part of the family, instead of the live–in handy–man. *It is to be expected,* she supposed. After all the child hadn't had a man role model in her life and sud-denly there was Joe Clay, bigger than life itself, right there in the house, sitting at the table right beside her. Mary just hoped when the remodeling was finished that Endora didn't go into a depression.

"Shhhh," Endora put her finger over her mouth and shushed her sisters. "We're going to surprise him."

"But Momma said to just knock and ask him," Rae said.

"Then that's what I'll do," Endora knocked so lightly her sisters had to strain to hear it and they were standing right beside her. Then she whispered, "Joe Clay, are you going to church with us? If you are then it's time to get up and come to breakfast."

"Guess he didn't hear me," Endora giggled as she slung the door open and rushed inside the bedroom, jumping in the middle of the king-sized bed and motioning the other girls to do the same.

"Wake up, Joe Clay. Wake up right now. It's time for breakfast and then you're going to church with us," Endora picked up a pillow and hit him in the face with it.

He sat straight up, coughing and sputtering, trying to get his bearings in the midst of four little girls. Merciful stars, was it really just eight o'clock? He hadn't come tip–toeing in from his poker game until six, barely two hours ago. He'd planned on staying in a hotel but changed his mind when he remembered the ladies would all be gone until at least noon with church services.

"I'm going back to sleep," he fell backwards and shut his eyes. Nothing moved. They should have hopped off the bed and slammed the door behind them. A minor distraction but he could go back to sleep.

"Joe Clay Carter, this is the Lord's day and you're going with us if I have to drag your hind end to church," Endora whispered in his ear.

"I'm not going to church. I am going back to sleep. Now

the bunch of you get out of my bedroom," he said without opening his eyes.

"Oh, yes, you are," Endora sing–songed into his ear, her blonde hair flowing over his face and tickling his nose. "If you want to go play cards all night with your buddies, that's fine, but this is the Lord's day and—"

"Endora Simmons!" Mary Jane exclaimed from the open door.

Joe Clay's eyes popped wide open and he pulled the sheet a little tighter over his bare chest. "She was just waking me up for church," he said.

"She was told to knock on your door and ask if you want-ed to join us," Mary Jane said.

"I did, but he was sleeping so good he didn't hear me," Endora said. "Didn't I knock on the door and ask him, Rae?"

"Yes, she did," Rae said, an angelic smile on her face.

"It's all right," Joe Clay said. "Give me five minutes and I'll be in for breakfast."

"Thank you," Endora whispered so light only Joe Clay heard it. Now the imp had him covering for her, but how could he let her get into trouble? *I just can't*, he kept telling himself as he dragged his weary body from bed and pulled on the t-shirt he'd worn to the poker game. He slipped his jeans up over his hips and zipped them but decided against the boots. He could eat breakfast in his bare feet and then he was coming right back to bed to sleep while the girls went to church.

They were waiting by the time he took his place at the head of the table.

"It's your turn Endora," Mary Jane said. She'd have a long talk with her four youngest daughters right after church. Good grief! Going into a man's bedroom like that. Could have been that he slept in the raw with no sheet.

"I'm passing my turn to Joe Clay this morning," Endora said.

Joe Clay cleared his throat and said a brief blessing for the food, wishing the whole time he'd sat right up in bed and told Mary Jane to keep her kids out of his room on his only day off. If he wanted to go to church, he'd be up and ready. If he didn't, then leave him alone.

"We missed you when we got home last night," Endora patted his arm. "This house didn't feel right without you in it. We found your note on the table and I guess it's all right if you go play cards with your friends, but you could have come home early."

"Endora! What Joe does on his time off is none of our business," Mary Jane chided.

"Why? What I do is everyone's business. It's Ursula's business because she's the oldest and it's Luna's because we share a room and it's yours because you're the Momma, so why can't Joe Clay's business be mine?" She asked innocently.

"Arguing before church ain't nice," Rae told her.

"Isn't," Mary Jane was ready to throw up her hands and put them all in their rooms for the rest of the day. Seeing Joe Clay wrapped in a sheet with all those little girls around him like he would be a real father had set her heart to beating entirely too fast. They did need a father, but it surely didn't need to be an opinionated ex–military man like Joe, and it did need to be someone that she could respect and admire. Maybe even love. And that's where the plot got sticky, because Mary Jane had given her heart away one time and it was thrown back at her in so many pieces it still hadn't been put back together. However, Joe Clay lying there with sleep in his eyes and covering up for Endora had been enough to make her want again. Want a man's arms around her at night while she drifted off into sleep. Want that feeling of euphoria when she walked into a room and his eyes lit up just looking at her.

But it wasn't going to happen with Joe Clay Carter. He'd be obliging when it came to put his arms around her at night, but come daylight he'd be gone. And his eyes might light up when she walked into the room, if she kept walking right into his arms, with no commitment. And happiness? That would be asking for the moon and stars to fall at her feet. She could never be happy with Joe Clay Carter. Not even if the past twenty years had softened up all that ego.

"Momma, you all right?" Ophelia asked.

Mary Jane blinked a couple of times and rejoined her family at the breakfast table. "I'm fine. Just wool gathering, I guess," she explained what must have been a blank look on her face.

"You wasn't gathering no wool," Luna said. "You were staring off into space like you saw a ghost. Did you? Did you see a ghost? What did it look like?"

"It looked like seven little girls with their hair all a mess," Mary Jane said, hoping if Joe Clay noticed the high color in her cheeks that he'd think it was leftover from the heat of the cook stove.

"Oh, Momma," Bo giggled. "Joe Clay, would you pass the sausage down here? Endora stop snarling like that. Just because you don't want to eat a pig, don't mean the rest of us don't."

"Why don't you eat meat?" Joe Clay asked, trying to steer the subject away from Mary Jane and her ghosts. Clearly she'd been lost in space somewhere. Thinking about that rascal of a husband and wishing she'd done something different so he'd be there to help her raise that passel of buttons and bows, he figured.

"Because I'm not eating something like Bambi or a sweet

little lamb or pig or calf," Endora said with a shudder. "I wouldn't want someone to have me for lunch."

"But they were put on the earth for us to eat. Don't you like the taste of a big old juicy Dairy Queen hamburger?" Joe Clay asked.

"Of course I do," Endora puffed out her chest and cheeks. "But it doesn't mean I'm going to eat one. Now if you'll hand me the peanut butter and honey, I'll have another waffle."

"That's too bad. I was thinking that after church, we might all go to the Dairy Queen in Nocona, get us a sack of hamburgers and go to the park. They've got this really neat park with tennis courts and lots of things to play on and we can't do any work around here on Sunday, so I'm told," he said.

"Really?" Endora said. Just like a real family with a momma and a daddy and a park. "Could we take a blanket and put it on the ground and eat on the blanket?" She asked.

"That's just the way I planned it," Joe Clay said. "But I don't imagine we'd better do that today because it takes a lot of energy to play on all those rides. Why it'd take more energy than one little old peanut butter waffle has got in it to just climb all the way to the top of the biggest slide. A little girl like you would plumb faint if she didn't have any protein in her body to give her enough energy to play."

"I guess I could eat just one hamburger if you think it's what I'd need to slide down that big old slide," Endora said very seriously. "Did you already ask Momma?"

"No, I didn't," Joe Clay said, suddenly tongue-tied. It wasn't like it was a date. Just a Sunday afternoon at the park on a blanket, most likely with him snoring a good deal of the time.

"Don't you think maybe you ought to?" Bo asked seriously.
Ursula held her breath. Ophelia crammed more waffles in

her mouth to prevent nervous giggles. Tertia stared at Mary Jane, unblinking. Rae and Bo held hands under the table. Luna grinned. Endora set her mouth just so and nodded at Joe Clay, giving him permission to ask her mother if they could go to the park.

"What would you think of that idea?" Joe Clay turned to Mary Jane. Good lord, he did believe she had worked on her aim all right. If looks could fire live ammo rounds, he would have been nothing more than a greasy spot on the kitchen floor. Of course, they had put her between a rock and a hard spot. If she refused, Endora didn't have to give up her vegetarian ways. If she accepted, she'd have to spend her only day off in the presence of Joe Clay and he wasn't foolish enough to think that was a top priority in her life. But by golly, it might do her some good. After all, he'd been rousted out of bed with the threat that Endora would drag his hind end to church.

"I think it's a wonderful idea. We'll come back here and change from our church clothes and spend the afternoon at the park. Hamburgers, fries and cokes. I'll even bring a picnic basket with cookies and extra drinks for mid-afternoon snacks," she smiled but it sure enough didn't reach her eyes. She hoped he spent eternity with Martin. Both of them shoveling coal into hell's furnace. She'd planned on spending the whole afternoon with the journals from the chest in the attic, not sharing a blanket with her handyman.

Mary Jane chose a summer dress of mint green from her closet. She twisted her hair up into a French roll and clamped it, letting the ends spike whichever way they wanted to go. She ran a hand up her legs, remembering that she had taken the time to shave them the night before, and dug out a pair of dark green sandals from the jumbled mass of shoes on the closet floor. A few quick strokes of makeup and the reflection in the mirror said she'd pass, even if she wouldn't win the Spanish Fort Beauty Contest that morning.

Joe Clay didn't own a suit. He hadn't been inside a church for anything but funerals and weddings in more years than he could remember. He'd worn his dress uniform to both his mother's and his father's funerals. The few weddings he had attended had been informal. So Endora would have to drag his hind end to church in crisply creased jeans and a white western-cut shirt. He knocked off two days worth of whiskers with a cordless electric razor and ran a dirty sock over his best pair of boots.

"Joe Clay," Endora's knock and voice came through the door. "Can you tie my sash?"

"Can I what?" He opened the door.

"Tie my sash. Momma is busy combing the rats out of Bo's hair. It's curly like Tertia's and Momma says it makes her lose her religion. Ursula was supposed to tie it for me but she's still getting dressed and won't let me in," Endora said.

"Turn around," Joe Clay said, taking the two long sashes in his hands. He flipped one over the other and drew them in to her waist. "Too tight?"

"Oh no, a lady must have a small waist. At least that's what Ophelia says. She says a girl can't be too skinny. I think she's wrong though. There's this girl in my room that looks like a broom stick she's so skinny. Make it a pretty bow or Momma will fuss," she told him seriously.

"Your Momma likes pretty bows, huh?" Joe Clay wrapped it just right and presto, a perfect bow.

"Yes, she does. Thank you Joe Clay. And you smell good. Can I hug you so I can smell whatever it is that you got on your face? I bet Momma would like that smell," Endora reached up for him to pick her up.

"You think so?" Joe Clay liked the feel of the child in his arms with her nose buried in his neck, inhaling deeply.

"Think so, what?" Mary Jane stepped around the corner.

"Oh, Momma, come here and smell Joe Clay's face. It smells just like heaven," Endora said.

"I don't have time to smell Joe Clay's cologne," Mary Jane felt a blush in the making and spun around to search her purse for keys.

"Can Joe Clay carry me out to the van and can he drive this morning?" Endora asked.

"Of course, I can," Joe Clay said. "Methinks there is a conspiracy afoot," he whispered to Mary Jane as he took the keys from her outstretched hands. "We'll have to have an executive officer's meeting later today."

"What?" Endora asked.

"Little corn has big ears," Mary Jane nodded.

"And there's lots of little corn in the field," Joe Clay told her.

"The wagon train leaves in two minutes," Mary Jane yelled up the stairs. A rumble raced down the stairs and out the door. "You don't really have to do this. I know you didn't get much sleep last night."

"Oh?" Joe Clay raised a dark eyebrow over sparkling blue eyes.

"I was up really early doing some research when I heard your truck," she explained as she crawled into the passenger seat of her van for the first time. She'd only bought it the year before and no one else had ever driven it. The world looked different from that seat even if it was only a couple of feet away from the steering wheel.

The only pew big enough to accommodate nine people was the very front one, so Mary Jane, Joe Clay, and seven little girls all paraded down the aisle to that very place. The preacher smiled at them, as if he were waiting on their appearance before he began services. "We're right glad to have Mary Jane Marsh and her family with us this morning. We're also glad to know that she's going to remodel that old historical house, one of the few original landmarks of Spanish Fort still left. Why, I'll bet we're the only town in the whole state of Texas who can boast that their population rose by more than ten percent in a single day," he chuckled.

"As most of you know Mary Jane is known in the writer's circles as M.J. Marsh and I understand she's got a full roster of books already in the process for next year. After services you can all make her and her family welcome. That would be her seven daughters and the man who's in charge of taking care of the remodeling project, Joe Carter. I'd like to extend our warmest welcome to you all. Now we'll sing, 'Blessed Redeemer'."

Endora found the hymn number the preacher said and held her book over to share with Joe Clay. Next time they all came to church together she'd have to be more careful and hurry on ahead to walk in with all her sisters. The way things had worked out that day, her mother led the way into the church with all the girls following behind her, Joe Clay bringing up the rear. They sat down just like they paraded inside. Next week, Endora would have to tell Ursula that they should hang back and make Joe Clay go in behind their mother. That way he'd have to share her hymn book.

Endora liked the singing but the preaching was a different matter. She tried crossing her eyes to make two of the preacher. It did give him four eyes and he looked sort of weird like that. Then she heard a little snort over to her left. Joe Clay was snoozing with his head on his chest. One solid pinch on his arm woke him right up with a jerk. She winked at him and nodded toward the preacher. She might not understand all those words, all the thees and thous he talked about out of the black book on his stand, but Joe Clay would if he stayed awake.

Everyone gathered round Mary Jane after services and wanted to welcome her. Richie, the boy in Ophelia's class, sidled up to her and whispered, "We don't have nuns in our church. I asked the preacher. So why are you here?"

"And I told you it's a big secret. We're going to be the first ones when we grow up. The President hasn't even told your preacher about it yet," Ophelia said with a shake of her red hair.

"The Pope has the say-so over nuns, not the President," Richie said.

"Not Baptist nuns," Ophelia told him. "That's the President's business, but keep your mouth shut or else the aliens will drop out of the sky and deduct you. They'll carry you away and make you a horse or a mule, then put you back down in the pasture behind my house. But don't worry, if I find you there I'll bring you carrots and take care of you. That's what all good Baptist nuns do."

Joe Clay bit the inside of his lip to keep from guffawing right there on the church lawn. No one ever had to worry about that child. She could hold her own with a whole den of wild coyotes. That little boy didn't have a snowball's chance in hell of getting ahead of her.

"Ready?" Mary Jane finally arrived at the van. "That was a real small town Texas welcome. I've been invited to sit on church committees, the PTA, to speak at the school about writing novels, and a dozen other things."

"Miss Popularity herself," Joe Clay said as he started up the engine and backed the car out away from the little white frame church.

"Oh, hush, it's just what I wanted when we came here. A small community where people were friendly. You ever lived in a big city?" She asked, then had the urge to slap herself across the face. Of course he'd been in big cities. He'd spent twenty years in the military and they didn't normally put their bases in towns with a total population of less than a hundred people.

"One or two, ma'am," he grinned. "There was San Diego, California. Then this little berg in Germany and that time I had to spend a year in Newport News, Virginia."

"I'm sorry," she leaned her head back and enjoyed being driven.

"No apology necessary. Those big cities, the traffic, and the indifference is what brought me home to Montague County, Texas," he said.

"Joe Clay, would you find me a puppy?" Bo asked out of the clear blue sky from the back seat. "We don't live in a big city no more and we've got a big yard and I want a puppy. Momma said we could have one someday. Could you talk her into getting me one soon?"

"A conspiracy afoot for sure," he mumbled. "Now Rae, that's between you and your momma, I'd say."

"I'm not Rae. I'm Bo. We're not identical so you should be able to tell us apart. I'm the one with the blue eyes. Rae's are green and she talks more than I do," Bo said.

"Do not," Rae said.

"That's enough. No fighting or we'll stay in today and you can all make peanut butter sandwiches for lunch," Mary Jane threatened. "And Bo, we'll talk about a puppy later. Maybe for Christmas."

"Rats!" Rae said.

"No. Puppies," Luna giggled.

"Here we are. Now let's see who can come out of these fancy duds the fastest and meet me back here at the car. Bet I can get this shirt off faster than any of you can change your dresses for shorts and t-shirts," Joe Clay expertly locked all the doors except the driver's with one click of the buttons on the door handle beside him, and then jumped out of the car to sprint toward the house.

"That's mean, Momma. Tell him that's no fair," Ursula yelled as she tried in vain to get out. "I coulda beat him. I know it but he cheated."

"That's the way with these men folk, girls. They'll side-step you every chance they get. Let that be a lesson to you. Take your time and let him stand out here in the hot sun and wait. Then we'll see who the smartest one is," Mary Jane laughed with them.

Joe Clay changed his good clothes for an old faded t-shirt and a pair of cut-off jeans. Using a boot jack he eased his feet out of his cowboy boots and slipped on a pair of athletic shoes with no socks. When they got to the park, he'd take the shoes off and take a nice long nap on the blanket. But for now, he intended to beat eight girls to the van. No way were a bunch of petticoats and fluff going to outdo a military man like Joseph Clayton Carter.

He waited ten minutes, checking his watch every few seconds. Endora was the first one to open the front door and meander out to the swing as if she had nowhere to go and all day to get there.

"Swing with me, Joe Clay," she patted the place beside her.

"And let them all come rushing out of the house and touch the van first?" He asked. "Is this a trick?"

"No, sir. But you're standing out there in the sun, sweating, and they're all upstairs fixing their hair and they don't even care if they beat you to the van," she smiled angelically.

"Rats!" He mocked Bo.

"No, puppies," she said.

He no more than parked his fanny on the swing when the

door flew open with an F-5 tornado force and a rush of girls tore across the lawn to pile into the van, Mary Jane giggling right along with them. He looked over to say something to Endora, only to find her seat empty and waving from the side window in the van. The big military hero had met his match.

"We got you!" They all said in unison when he got behind the wheel.

"Endora is a witch," he said, a grin tickling the corners of his mouth as he looked at Mary Jane.

"I believe she was on that old television show "Bewitched." Wasn't she the mother–in–law who turned Elizabeth Montgomery's husband into a frog or a donkey?"

"Well, that little witch back there sure turned me into one. A first rate donkey," he said. "You won that one, but you just remember paybacks are . . ." he stumbled over the word the guys used, ". . . paybacks are very unpleasant."

"Yes, they are," Mary Jane nodded. She couldn't remember the last time she'd had so much fun, but she couldn't let it give her a case of flutters. Joe Clay would be gone in a few months and she'd be right back where she was when she moved to Spanish Fort.

They picked up hamburgers and fries at the Dairy Queen and took them to the Nocona Park, where the younger four girls could hardly swallow fast enough. The little rides, the slide, the swings all beckoned to them. The older three girls, Ursula, Ophelia, and Tertia brought their tennis gear to work on their games. As soon as the last french fry was wolfed down, they all disappeared in a flash, leaving Mary Jane and Joe Clay on the blanket alone.

"I can't believe you got her to eat meat," Mary Jane worked at picking up the mess and cramming it down into a paper bag. "She hasn't touched it in months."

"All a matter of what she wants more. To play or to stay home and read a book," Joe Clay took off his shoes and laid flat on his stomach, using his muscular arms for a pillow. "Wake me when they're tired."

"Oh, no. You brought us out here. So when they get ready for someone to push them or make the merry–go–round go faster you can keep your eyes open and help. Besides, they'll just wake you up anyway. Don't you know this is part of that conspiracy that's afoot?"

"I know. They're plotting to get us together. Hell if I know why they like me, but they do. I hate kids and girls are worse than boys. Evidently they haven't had much luck with setting you up with a husband and getting a daddy for themselves in the deal. Even someone with gray hair and a scar on his face is looking good these days," he said, opening his eyes a slit to see how she'd take that bit of news.

"I'm not interested. And I don't think there's a united front, just a few mismatched incidents," Mary Jane said. "They've been pretty content with the status quo. Their father comes at Christmas from wherever he and Miss Bimbo are living at the time. I understand she has a house, complete with servants in every country in the world. That part in the Good Book where it says the gospel shall find its way into every corner of the world. Well, her money is ahead of the gospel. Anyway, they talk to him on the phone about once a month and he sees them one night and one day at Christmas. Other than Luna's dentist, they haven't tried any shenanigans before now."

"Then maybe Endora really does like me. You know I tied her sash this morning," Joe Clay said.

"That little minx," Mary Jane shook her head in bewilderment.

"So you think there's not a mutiny, just a few happenings that are disconnected?" he asked.

"They do like you in spite of the fact you don't like them," Mary Jane said.

"I didn't say I didn't like them. I don't like kids, not them. They're not kids. They're people," he shut his eyes. Maybe just a few winks before one of them came in a full out rush begging for a fast merry–go–round.

"Well," Mary Jane sucked up a chest full of air to tell him that she appreciated his setting her kids in a different category, but before she could get out more than one word, he was snoring. She picked up her satchel and took out the second journal, the one where Miss Raven talked about the sheriff, with the gray in his temples and that swash-buckling stance, along with his blue eyes which gave her a case of vapors every time he stepped up on her porch. The story would practically write itself when she got back to her computer on Monday morning.

Chapter Six

There was nothing prettier in the whole world than a Texas sunset. Especially one where the earth looked flat, where the dirt and sky met each other and the sun simply fell off the side of the world. Oranges competed with yellows and pinks to put on a show more brilliant than a fresh new box of crayons. Mary Jane rocked herself in the porch swing and enjoyed the fresh air, the sunset, the end of another Saturday.

Ursula was upstairs, putting her room together with Ophelia's help. Not that Ophelia didn't have ulterior motives. Her reconstruction was next and the sooner she got things out of her room, the sooner Joe Clay could begin his job. Ophelia had already moved all her belongings into Tertia's room. The plan was that Ophelia would share Tertia's room, then Tertia would move in with Bo and Rae when her turn came. When she was back in her room, Bo and Rae would move in with Luna and Endora. By the time it was Luna and Endora's turn, the spare room would be almost empty and they'd use it until their room was finished.

At the moment Tertia had spread a blanket out under the mimosa tree in the side yard and was reading a book. Jenny B. Jones was the new love of her life and she'd collected every one of them. Today, while they'd been shopping she'd found the latest and could hardly sit still long enough to get home and claim a quiet spot to read. The other four were making enough noise to pollute the entire county with their squeals as they jumped and did acrobatics on the trampoline in the back yard.

Mary Jane reached out and ran the tip of her finger across the scraped wood on the front of the porch. The boys had done a fine job, finishing the scrapping just that day. She'd met Joe Clay leaving as she and the girls came home from a day in Gainesville. In three weeks, they had the day down to a flexible routine. First the outlet mall for a little shopping. Lunch. Today it was Tertia's turn to choose the place and she'd decided on fajitas from Chili's. Then a matinee at the movies. Shopping at Wal–Mart for groceries and supplies and back home for a make–do supper of sandwiches.

She stopped swinging and stared at the layers of paint the boys had scraped away, leaving little pockets where every color could be seen. There was the original grainy wood showing down deep. She leaned forward, thinking about the time when the house was built—1874. Miss Raven, an English woman who'd come to Texas, saw a business opportunity and had it built. The wood that Mary Jane could see at the base of the layers of paint had been standing in this location more than a hundred years.

She began to swing again. Her book was coming along fast and furious. Almost as if it had a mind of its own and only used her fingertips and computer monitor as tools to bring it to life. Her editor had already begun to talk to her about it being the first of a series. The next seven would be the stories of the seven women who worked with Miss Raven in Paradise, and the title had changed several times. Now the whole series was called *The Angels of Paradise*. The first one would be *A Visit to Paradise*. From the first time the sheriff paid his money for a night in Paradise, he'd fallen in love with Miss Raven. By the end of the book, they will be married. But what happened to those other seven fallen angels? Each one had a story and even though it was only a sentence or two in the journal where Miss Raven recorded the last time the Paradise was open for business, it was enough to provide fodder for the romance mill for at least eight books. Mary Jane still hadn't put her signature on the line that said she'd write an eight book series, but she was going to do it. Norm was seeing dollar signs in the sky. Already he was talking television mini–series and Oprah.

She wondered what the Taovaya Indians would think of that, if they were still around. They were the Indians who'd first occupied the area, way back in 1759, according to her research. The tribe was decimated by the smallpox, who couldn't hold out against American settlers who claimed the area for their new town. The Taovayas who gave up fighting even with their Spanish cannon and headed west to merge with the Wichitas. *Is there another book there*? She wondered. One of a Taovaya princess who stayed behind to marry an American settler.

Then came the Chisolm Trail through Spanish Fort, and Miss Raven saw the possibility of making big money. Mary Jane didn't figure she'd planned on losing her heart to the sheriff though. Of all the people in the booming town, sporting four hotels, several saloons, a doctor, and a couple of other bordellos, Miss Raven would have never thought when she had the first coat of white paint put on the house that fate had already thrown her and the sheriff together.

Then there was the white paint. Mary Jane wondered how long it lasted before someone painted it that hideous shade of gray. Perhaps when the railroad made transporting the cattle an easier job. Maybe it was when Miss Raven died and her daughter took over the place, farming the acreage around it. The next time it was painted the owners chose a pale yellow. Could that have been when the oil boom poured a little money back into Spanish Fort? Back in the early 1920s when there'd been enough interest to even warrant building the old school. After that it was gray again and then the horrid turtle–dung green. So many layers, but so many stories.

Just like your heart, a little voice said from somewhere deep inside her heart. She gazed again at the spot where all the colors were visible. Raw wood. Like she was in the beginning. Green. Naive. Then a coat of pure white. Like her marriage to Martin. Everything was perfect. White covered a world where no black existed. Then the nasty old gray paint called divorce spilled out over every emotion she had. That was followed by the light yellow when she woke up and realized she had seven precious little girls who needed her. But after a couple of years the gray came back, reminding her there was no one for her, no one to share the moments when Ophelia brought home a perfect report card; when Rae won the talent contest in her grade; when Ursula picked out her first bra. Now the turtle–dung green showing in big wide patches. What was that? It was Dallas, Texas. The crappy big city life she'd left behind to move to something slower. And now it was time to cover all those layers back up with the original white. But what did that signify?

A rumble followed by a trail of dust, not totally unlike the boiling leftovers from the real cattle drive, brought Joe Clay's pickup truck down the lane and into the front yard. His gray hair was covered with a dull powdery dust. His shirt a challenge for any Tide commercial. His jeans even worse.

"Bathroom empty?" He asked as he crossed the yard.

Did Miss Raven's heart skip a beat when Sheriff Parilla's boots made the same noise on the wooden porch? Mary Jane wondered. Of course Miss Raven was now Miss Sarah and Sheriff Parilla had become Sam Prentice. All characters and places are fiction and any resemblance to actual people, living or dead, is purely coincidental. The resemblance was there, but Mary Jane had coated it with pure fiction until even Miss Raven would have problems recognizing herself. For one thing she wasn't an English woman sent to the United States as punishment, and she surely was pure at heart, keeping her room empty for only Jim Prentice.

"Did you hear me?" Joe Clay asked.

"I'm sorry. I was wool gathering again. Yes, the bathroom is open. Both upstairs and downstairs, unless either Ursula or Ophelia is in one of them. They're working on Ursula's room. I didn't expect to see you tonight," she said.

"I'm going for a shower right now. I feel like half of the dirt in Texas is hugging me like a brother," he disappeared into the house.

Fifteen minutes later, a different Joe Clay emerged. Clean t-shirt and cut-off jean shorts. Bare feet. Gray hair sparkling. Smelling like heaven. He sat down on the swing beside Mary Jane. "We got to the end of the job so I paid the boys time and a half for an extra hour to finish up today. That way the painters can begin Monday morning. One of the kids needed a ride home so I took him. Wasn't expecting you girls home until after dark."

"We caught the early matinee today and there wasn't much we needed at the Wal–Mart store," she said.

"Evidently you missed this," he reached over against the house and set a can of corn between them.

"Sack broke. The last one. Scattered can goods all over the porch," she explained. "The boys did a really good job of scraping this old place down. And the new porch looks good, Joe Clay. It feels sturdy on the feet."

"What color do you want it? White's not a good color for a porch," he said. "You don't have to make up your mind today, but be thinking on it."

"Porches were usually either brown or gray in the time period when the house was built. I hate brown. So a neutral shade of gray would be good," she hoped that wouldn't be an omen to cover her heart in a gray fog again. No, that was pure silliness. The house with its coats of many colors certainly was not a parallel to her own existence. It had just been something to think about as the sun set on a Texas day.

"Okay, then gray it will be, which reminds me of something else gray. I'll go put on my shoes and I want you to see something," he said.

"What would that be?" She asked.

"A surprise, but only if you want it to be," he told her. "They're your kids. Good kids that almost make me want to change my mind about all kids in general. But a day with a bunch of hormonal teenage boys can sure enough keep me from doing that."

In a few minutes he returned, shoes on his feet, a glass of tea in his hand. "Come on. The surprise is out in the garage."

He led the way but she walked beside him. Ursula and Ophelia watched from the upstairs window. Tertia peeked out over the top of her book and smiled. Four little girls on the trampoline yelled even louder.

"You been building something special in here?" Mary Jane asked.

"Haven't had time for anything more than remodeling, not that I wouldn't like to build something special. Always had it in mind I'd put together a complete bedroom suit out of red oak. Big old sleigh bed, triple dresser, chest of drawers, night stands, maybe even a matching entertainment unit to hold the bedroom television set. But it'll take a big room to hold that much furniture. No, it's not a building project I've brought you to see. It's something a lot simpler. Just a decision on your part and saving the price of a puppy out of your checkbook," he said.

"Now you've really piqued my curiosity," she laughed.

A nice sound. Mary Jane's laughter. He'd listened to it several times over the past three weeks. When she'd been spending time with her girls. It was the first time he'd heard it when it was just the two of them. At least sincere laughter. There'd been a few times when she'd chuckled in derision.

They stepped into the darkened garage and he flipped a switch, lighting up a bare bulb hanging from the ceiling.

"She's over here in the corner, on an old toe sack. I found her this morning. She's tame as she can be. Way I figure it is someone tossed her out, knowing she was about to explode and she found her way to the best place," he pointed at a gray cat, curled around a nest of furry kittens.

"Oh, my!" Mary Jane stooped down to rub the mother cat's ears. She got a deep purr for her attention. "Kittens. Bo wanted either a kitten or a puppy."

"I know. It's all I've heard for two weeks. Every time she gets a chance she's under my feet begging me to ask you to get her one or the other. Well, this old girl just dropped five kittens. Now that's two short of a full house. That'd be one for each of the girls, but I figure maybe there could be some sharing, and I don't think Ursula or Ophelia are so dead set on having one." Joe Clay's heart was so light it floated right out of his chest to hover over Mary Jane and that old momma cat.

"We can't leave them in the garage. I've heard coyotes in the night. We'd have to have a full-fledged funeral with flowers and a minister if one of them died after the girls have seen them," she said.

"Then you're going to let them keep them? I'd thought if you decided against adopting the whole bunch, I'd just load them up in the truck tonight after they've gone to bed. I can take them to the shed out back of my folks' place. Renters wouldn't mind if I kept them in food to take out to the momma cat," he said.

"I don't think I'm adopting them. I think this old girl has adopted us. Yes, they can keep them. We'll have to take them into the utility room. There's room at the end of the washing machine to put a laundry basket and an old blanket. That would work, wouldn't it, for a few weeks? By then they'll have them in every room of the house," Mary Jane said. "Oh, look, there's an orange one. I had an orange kitten when I was a little girl."

"So is that one your new cat?" Joe Clay asked.

"No, the momma cat is mine," Mary Jane said. "Think we can sneak them into the house and oh, no . . . we'll have to wait until I can go into town and buy kitty litter."

"I picked up some on my way back from taking Tim home. Just in case, you know, that you'd say the magic yes word," Joe said sheepishly.

"Joe Clay Carter, did you also just happen to tote this momma cat out here and put her in this garage?" She popped her hands on her hips and glared at him, her nose only three inches from his.

"I did not. She just showed up and that's the God's honest truth," he declared.

One moment he was glaring right back at her. The next his eyes shut and his mouth was firmly on hers, tasting onions and peppers from picante sauce. Feeling the earth shake slightly under his feet, and an ache in his heart that hadn't been there before.

One second she was ready to change her mind about the cats, to tell him she didn't trust him as far as she could throw him, that he'd just brought the cat there to get Rae off his back. The next, her eyes were shut and she was enjoying a kiss straight from one of her romance novels. Her body leaned into his and her arms, with a mind of their own, wrapped around his neck. Somewhere in the distance she heard a cat purring so loud it hummed in her heart like a constant vibration.

"What was that all about?" She bristled when the kiss ended, a flush starting in the pits of her stomach and radiating outward, finally reaching her face to heat it up to a rich scarlet color.

"Just a kiss. Spur of the moment," he said hoarsely. He'd known twenty years ago there was chemistry between them. Known it down deep in his heart, but hadn't had any idea then just how much. Now he knew, and the pain of not having it was probably going to be the hardest thing he'd ever face. The famous M.J. Marsh wouldn't be interested in plain old Joseph Clayton Carter. Not for anything other than rewiring and hanging sheet rock. And that job would be done in a few months. He wished he'd never given in to his impulses and kissed her. Wished he could take back the past three minutes and rewrite the history of it.

"Well don't give in to the spur of the moment again," she said briskly, covering up her own trembling soul. What she'd just experienced only lived in books. Real people didn't get that kind of spark from a kiss. "I'm going to distract the girls. Call them into my room to discuss tomorrow's Sunday school lesson. There's an empty laundry basket on the top of the dryer. If you'll bring the kittens and the momma cat to the utility room, then we'll let Bo find them."

"How do you plan on doing that?" He stepped back another foot, but the heat between them was still hotter than even the September night breezes.

"By asking her to go find me a pair of socks out of the dryer or some such thing," Mary Jane said. "And Joe Clay, the kiss was nice. Very nice. It's just that we don't want the same things and it's a shame to waste time on something that has no future."

"Thank you, ma'am," he bowed deeply, trying to regain the light-hearted feeling they'd shared when she first saw the cat and kittens.

"Don't tease. I'm trying to be adult," she said.

"I know, Mary Jane. Now go divert the kids and we'll forget the kiss," he said.

Yeah right. The first time I've been kissed in four years. The first time I've ever been kissed like that. Even Martin's passionate kisses in the beginning of our relationship didn't heat me up like that, she thought as she stomped toward the house.

"Hey, come on inside," she motioned to the four still out on the trampoline. Tertia's blanket was gone from under the mimosa tree so when she stepped into the house, she added her name to the other two, calling them all into her bedroom.

"What's going on?" Ursula asked. She'd watched her mother go into the garage with Joe Clay and then the way she stomped across the yard when she left alone. Rather than going out there alone and maybe something romantic happening, they'd had a big fight. "Did you fire Joe Clay?"

"Oh, no!" Ophelia laid the back of her hand on her forehead, pure Scarlett O'Hara style and moaned. "Now my room will never be finished. What am I to do?"

"I didn't fire Joe Clay. We were just having a discussion about this remodeling," Mary Jane justified her lie by thinking that she was remodeling their lifestyle. Adding six cats to it. If that didn't fall under the change of habit, nothing would.

"Thank goodness!" Ophelia sighed in relief. "Now what did you want with all of us at once, Momma?"

"Have you all studied for your Sunday school lessons?" She asked.

"Noooo," came seven voices.

"Well, you'll need to do that after a while. I suppose you've all got different ones?" She asked.

"Ophelia and I go to one class and the other four go to another," Ursula said. "So there's two different classes. Want me to go up and get our books?"

"No," Mary Jane said hurriedly. "Sit down and talk to me a bit. We've all been so busy we haven't had time to talk."

"Momma, we just spent the whole day together," Tertia told her with a sigh. "What is going on that you've got to keep us all in one room? Did Joe Clay quit his job and you're waiting for him to leave before you tell us?"

"Oh, no, I take back the praises," Ophelia threw her hand across her forehead again.

"Joe Clay didn't quit. As far as I know he's staying on the job until it's finished. Until Christmas. Then we'll have a wonderful Christmas in Paradise with your Aunt Maggie and her family and Uncle Ross and his family. Grandma and Gramps Marsh are coming for two or three days in their camper and we'll decorate the new house with so many lights they can see them all the way from Dallas," she said.

"You can have the praises back," Ophelia raised a hand

again. "Like the Griswolds' house, Momma? Can we have that many lights?"

"Sure you can. We'll put red bunting on the upstairs balcony with lights all in it. Maybe even a fake tree on the front porch, and we'll decorate the trees around here with lights," she said, getting into the spirit three months ahead of time.

"Even the ones down the lane?" Endora asked.

"Even the ones down the lane. Before Joe Clay leaves, I'll tell him to fix an electrical system so we can throw a switch and light us up just like the Griswolds'," she laughed.

"Excuse me," Joe Clay yelled through the door as he knocked.

"You sure he's staying? I'd miss him an awful lot if he left and I'm sure I could never eat another hamburger if Joe Clay left," Endora threatened.

"He's staying," Mary Jane whispered. "Come on in. We're all in here." She yelled toward the door.

He cautiously peeked inside and stepped across the threshold into her sanctuary. A king-sized bed, dresser, books strewn around the floor, seven girls on the bed with her. "Just thought I'd let you all know that I'm going into town for a card game and won't be back until tomorrow evening."

"But you can't," Endora threw herself into his arms. "I told my friend you'd be in church with us tomorrow. She said you looked like an actor in a movie she saw on television last weekend and she wanted to see you again so she could be sure. Please come back to go to church with us."

"Endora, Mr. Carter has got a life of his own. He only gets one day off from work and being around a bunch of girls. We can't ask him to give that up," Mary Jane said.

"Yes, I can," Endora said. "I like it when we all go into the church together. It's the one time I feel like I've got a whole family."

Joe Clay was tongue-tied even more than he'd been after the kiss in the garage. Someone needed him. Really needed him. He'd been needed in his lifetime. Needed as a son to late-life parents who were in their mid-forties when he was born. Needed as a leader, in so many military actions he couldn't even count them, to bring his men through the mission safely. But never needed to make a whole family. Yet, if he gave in to Endora's whim, it would just make the leaving harder at Christmas. If he didn't, he'd break her heart and he loved her too much for that.

Loved her? The two words echoed in his mind like they'd been spoken from the bottom of the Grand Canyon. Loved an impish blonde-haired, blue-eyed kid. He'd have to think about that later. For now, he wasn't going to break her heart.

"Is that an invitation?" He looked at Endora.

"Oh, yes, it is," she leaned back and looked into his eyes. "Did you ever notice how much our eyes are alike, Joe Clay? Why if I didn't know from the DPA that my daddy was the same as Ursula's and all the rest of them, I could think you were my daddy."

"Now that's just plain silly," Joe Clay grinned. "I'm too mean and hateful to be anyone's daddy. That's why I don't have kids. Besides, I don't like kids."

"You can fool some folks by saying that," Endora giggled. "But not me."

"Mission accomplished," Joe Clay mouthed at Mary Jane who for some strange reason was blushing.

"Bo, would you go out and get me a pair of socks from the dryer. White ones, please," Mary Jane asked.

"What for? You got dirty feet from walking out to the garage with Joe Clay. You can't put white socks on dirty feet," Bo said.

"Just please mind me. I didn't say I was going to put them

on right now. I just want them brought to me," she said in exasperation.

"I'll do it, Momma," Luna bounced across the bed.

Mary Jane barely grabbed her shirttail in time to keep her from running down the stairs and to the utility room. "No, I want Bo to go. She's the one I asked."

"Okay," Bo sighed. "Why me? Luna could go. Just one pair of socks or do you want me to bring the whole load? We could sort them. Joe Clay could help us."

"Oh, no you don't," Joe Clay put Endora back on the bed and put up his hands. "I hate sorting socks and Endora might talk me into church, but a dozen angels playing their harps and singing 'Red Hot Momma' just like Trace Atkins couldn't make me sort socks."

"Okay then," Bo snorted.

Mary Jane let her get halfway down the stairs when she whispered to the other girls to hurry up and follow her. There was a surprise in the utility room. But let her find it first. Excitement radiated from the walls as they crept down the stairs; Joe Clay and Mary Jane a few feet behind them.

"Oh! Oh! Oh!" They heard Bo's voice, high and squeaky, when she discovered the laundry basket full of cats. "Momma, come quick. I think Santa Claus came early."

The other girls swooped in like a hot September breeze, their whoops and hollers loud enough to wake up the dead. Joe Clay slipped his arm around Mary Jane's waist as they watched from the doorway. It felt right to be there and she didn't push it away in the melee of oohs and ahhs that flowed all around the room.

"Can we pick them up?" Bo asked.

"I wouldn't today," Joe Clay said. "Give the momma cat time to adjust to her surroundings. If you handle them too early, she'll move them and you won't get to play with them at all."

"How many are there? It looks like a bunch of little fur balls." Endora asked.

"Five kittens, so you'll have to share. Joe Clay found them in the garage this morning," Mary Jane suddenly realized he had his arm around her. She shook it off and stooped down to peer inside the basket with her daughters.

"I don't need one to be mine, personally," Ursula said. "I'll just pet them all equally."

"I do," Rae said. "And I want that orange one."

"I think Bo should get first choice," Mary Jane told them. "She's the one who has been asking for a pet."

"She can have the orange one," Bo said. "I don't care which one is mine, just so long as I get one. Everyone else can pick first when we can see them and I'll take the last one. That way the least favorite one will get the most love, because my cat is going to be loved more than any of them."

"I don't need a special one either. I'm just glad Joe Clay didn't quit out there in that garage and I get my own room. Besides I'd rather have a horse. Think you could find one of those in the garage, Joe Clay?" Ophelia asked.

Mary Jane rolled her eyes.

Joe Clay threw back his head and roared.

Chapter Seven

Dawn reached out her long orange fingers, giving definition to trees, yelling at the population of Spanish Fort to arise. *Get up and going. Today is Sunday. Inhale the sweet summer air once more. Get ready for church.* Joe Clay stretched and threw the sheet off just about the time his cell phone played "Dixie." He grabbed for it, thinking it was most likely his poker buddies, just breaking up the game, razing him about losing out on a wonderful game.

"Mr. Carter, I'm sorry to call you this early but we've got a problem with your rent house. Your folks' home. It's burning to the ground," a slightly familiar voice said.

"Is the renter out?" Joe Clay asked.

"Yes, he wasn't home. We're trying to get it under control but it's pretty hot," the man said.

"I'm on my way," Joe Clay held the phone on his shoulder and dressed even as he spoke. In less than three minutes he'd pulled on his jeans, boots, and a fresh t-shirt, and was out the door before he realized he hadn't let the girls know where he was going. He went back inside, borrowed a piece of notebook paper from the first backpack on the floor beside the foyer table and hurriedly wrote:

Trouble with my rent house. Back as soon as possible.
                                                           JC

"Hey Joe Clay, man, we're right sorry about this. We're still shooting water in there but it looks like it's going to be a total loss," Pete, the fireman, a distant cousin of Joe's yelled when he arrived on the scene.

Two pickup trucks emblazoned with Nocona Police Department on the side, two fire trucks, and a host of onlookers were outside his old family home. He could scarcely believe the blaze. He'd expected that old house to stand as long as the Paradise had. His folks had it built back in the middle forties, the first year they were married. He'd planned to move back into it at Christmas and begin remodeling it. Maybe fate was telling him that he had no permanent place in Montague County, Texas.

"What can I do to help?" He asked Pete.

"Not a thing. We're just trying to contain the blaze so the wind doesn't carry the hot ash over to the neighbor's place. We've already wet down the yard and bushes over there. It's pretty hot. 'Bout all we can do is wait until it cools off enough to figure out what caused it. Got in touch with the renter. He's been down in Denton with his folks for the weekend," Pete told him.

So he stood there in a trance, thirty-eight years flashing through his mind. His mother, picking apples from the tree right off the back porch which was a part of the blaze. He and his father picking up pecans and then sitting around the kitchen table picking them out so his mother could make pecan pies for Thanksgiving. The smell of fresh bread on

Wednesday afternoons when he came home from school. His mother in her Sunday best dress and hat, complete with white gloves, at his high school graduation. The way she kissed him, tears in her eyes at the front door, when he left to join the military. The sight of his father sitting in that old worn recliner and nodding his head in agreement when Joe Clay came home on leave to tell him he'd decided to stay in the service for the long haul. Thanksgiving. Always Thanksgiving. His mother's favorite holiday. The time when they all came home. He'd come from halfway around the world more than once just to spend Thanksgiving with his family.

He'd buried them both, within six months of each other, five years ago. He'd put the things he couldn't bear to part with in storage and rented the house to a single man who worked at the school. His father's recliner, in bad need of reupholstery. His mother's pump organ. Boxes and boxes of sentimental items. But now those things had no place to call home again. Joe Clay stood with his hands deep in his pockets watching fire bury his past and future.

Mary Jane and the girls were early enough that Sunday morning to garner a pew halfway back in the church. Endora had been more than a little disappointed when she found out Joe Clay wasn't coming with them, *but that's good for her*, Mary Jane thought. He'd be gone in less than three months. It was best she suffer a little disappointment now than have a big platter of it served up to her all at once.

Several people stopped to talk to Mary Jane after services again so she and the girls were the last ones to shake hands with the preacher, who stood at the door, greeting each person as they left. "Wonderful sermon this morning," she told him.

Instead of shaking her hand and letting go with a polite nod or even a few words, he held it in both of his. "I'd like to ask you and the girls to allow me to take you to lunch today. Perhaps over to Gainesville. Chili's. Applebees. You name the place and provide a vehicle big enough to tote us and I'll treat you all. My little pickup truck wouldn't hardly haul all of us, unless the girls wanted to ride in their Sunday finery in the back. And I'm afraid that the law says that's a big no–no," he said.

He was as tall as Mary Jane when she wore flat-soled shoes. If she'd put on her high heels, he would have been looking at her chin rather than into her eyes. He had a pleasant round baby face with little sign of a beard and the same color brown eyes as his thin hair. Wireless glasses perched on his small nose and his mouth was thin. His voice, though, was deep and his smile genuine.

"How about we all go back to Paradise and have lunch?" She withdrew her hand from his firm grasp. "The girls have a new litter of baby kittens and they'll be wanting to keep close check on them this afternoon, and I'd be glad to have you join us at our table. Don't expect much out of Paradise right now. We're remodeling and I'm afraid the kitchen is the last room on the agenda."

"Well, thank you and yes, I would be glad to share a meal with you. But I have to warn you, I'm a vegetarian. I do eat dairy but not meat," he said.

"Not a problem. I've already made lasagna. One with meat; one vegetarian. Endora likes hers that way, too," she said.

"How wonderful!" He clapped his hands together. "One of the girls and I will see eye–to–eye about eating anything that had a face."

"Semi," Mary Jane said. "She eats Dairy Queen hamburgers when she needs lots of energy. And last week she did manage to consume a whole chicken leg but that's because Joe Clay told her the running gear on the chicken was his favorite part. She really likes him a lot."

"Well, we'll see about that," Pastor Frances McSwain said. "Shall I follow you in my truck then?"

"That would be just fine," Mary Jane nodded.

"You invited the preacher for dinner? Why'd you go and do that? Joe Clay will probably be home and where will the preacher man sit? He's not going to sit beside me, is he? You're not going to ask him to say the prayer, are you? He'll pray forever and what if Joe Clay doesn't like him?" Endora kept a steady flow of questions flying around in the van.

"Yes, I invited him to dinner, but that's because he issued an invitation to all of us to go to Gainesville and eat at a restaurant. That would have meant you girls had to keep your Sunday finery on all day and be very nice even if you didn't like him. When he's at our house, you can go off and do your own thing after dinner. Yes, I suppose if Joe Clay isn't back, he will sit at that end of the table right beside you, Endora, and you will be nice. If he prays until the lasagna gets stone cold, you will be nice. And it doesn't matter one bit if Joe Clay doesn't like him. It's my house and I'll invite whomever I please for Sunday dinner. Joe Clay is just the hired help and he'll be leaving in a few months, so you might as well face it right now. I know you like him but that's only because there's been no other man about the house as much as he's been. It's only natural that you'd take up with him, especially when he's nice to you. But the whole bunch of you need to realize that he's already let it be known he really doesn't like kids. If he'd wanted a family he would have started one long ago. He's a nice man and he's wonderful at his job, but he's not up for grabs as a surrogate father, Endora," Mary Jane said.

"Is the preacher?" Bo asked from right behind Mary Jane.

"No! He is not. And I'm not looking for a husband. I've got seven daughters and my writing. That's enough to keep me busy until I'm old and gray," Mary Jane said in pure exasperation.

"Good," Rae said. "I think he's all right as a preacher but I don't think I'd want him around for more than an hour."

Ophelia poked Rae in the leg and grinned at her. Then she said, "Well, I suppose if he wants to court Momma, I could live with the idea. You know, it might be nice to have a preacher in the family. Then I could tell Richie that the President said Momma could marry him so we could raise up a house full of Baptist nuns."

Mary Jane rolled her eyes in bewilderment. "The preacher is not here to court me. I'm not interested in him that way. He's our minister and this is not a courting type call. It's Sunday dinner with the preacher. People invite the preacher to dinner all the time. Probably no one thought to ask him today so he was being cordial and asking us so he wouldn't have to eat alone."

"Does he know how much it costs to invite all of us to dinner?" Ursula asked. "Are preachers rich?"

"Not that I know of," Mary Jane parked the van in front of the house. "Now the bunch of you. Best behavior today. You may change clothes before lunch if you want, but I'll expect perfect manners."

"Yes ma'am," Ursula answered for all of them.

Frances McSwain stepped out of his beige Chevrolet S–10 pickup and took stock of the place. He'd done his homework last week when he'd been called to preach one Sunday at the Spanish Fort church. The Paradise was an old bordello back in the cattle drive days and had been passed down to the oldest daughter for generations. Until the last one died with no heirs. Then M.J. Marsh bought it to get out of the big city life. She was having it remodeled, expenses not even considered. He'd heard that she had a bathroom upstairs with two tubs and showers and seven pink sinks. One for each daughter. Her hired hand lived in the house with them, but his quarters were on the ground floor. She and the girls all had rooms on the second floor. There was talk that if it took a million dollars she intended to have it all done by Christmas.

By spring Frances envisioned himself spraying those pecan trees lining the lane. He'd be putting in a circular driveway with crape myrtles, vinca major, and English ivy. In a year rose bushes and clematis would vine up the porch posts. Maybe a bed of peonies all around the porch and creeping phlox to give the place color. It would look like a vision from a Thomas Kincaid painting.

Oh, yes, Frances could see a great future. And when the girls were all grown, they could open the upstairs up to a bed and breakfast enterprise. Mary Jane could give up her little romance novels and cook for the guests. He could sit on the porch and play the part of the southern gentleman, telling them all about the history of the whole area. He already saw himself in a white suit and a straw hat. Oh yes, Frances could play that part very well.

Mary Jane wasn't a raving beauty but she was the mother of seven children. One couldn't expect her to look like a teenager, now could they? She would do fine for a wife and daughter–in–law to his sweet mother.

"Welcome to Paradise," Ursula said right at his elbow.

"Well, thank you my child. But really now, don't you think you should say, 'our home,' instead of Paradise? After all that has a bit of an ugly connotation to it. People tend to remember why it was built when you say that. Perhaps a new name should go with the remodeling. Something like Twelve Oaks or Whispering Pines," he said.

"You'll have to talk to Momma about that. Right now, it's just Paradise," Ursula smiled brightly. This man would be lucky to last until dessert was served. "Hey, girls, Momma said we could change into our shorts. Let's all go upstairs. Meet you in my room in five minutes."

That was the cue. One minute the porch was filled with giggles, ruffles, and frills, the next the only people in the unkept, grassless yard were Frances and Mary Jane.

"I'm a bit of a gardener. Love to piddle and create beauty out of the wilds. Someday we'll have to talk about what you need to do to make this yard fit for the *Better Homes and Garden* magazine," he said.

"That would be wonderful," she said. "Now welcome to our home, the Paradise. Have a seat on the porch swing while I put the finishing touches on lunch. Or come on inside and sit at the table and watch me. Or would you like something cold to drink and the Sunday paper to read while you wait in the living room?"

He followed her through the front door. "I think I'll take you up on the second offer. Maybe a glass of tea would be nice while we visit as you finish lunch."

Mary Jane set her purse on the foyer table and went straight back to the kitchen. She would have liked to change into cut-off jeans and an oversized sleeveless shirt but since Preacher McSwain was in a three-pieced suit, she guessed she'd best stay in her dress. At least it was sleeveless and she wasn't wearing panty hose.

"I'll just pop these into the oven for half an hour. Then

while they cool enough to cut, I can bake the hot rolls." She pulled two pans of lasagna and one of yeasty rolls from the refrigerator. "Now I'll fix you a glass of tea."

She reached for the glass jug on the counter and a clean glass from the cabinet. "Bama crystal will have to do, I'm afraid. I haven't unpacked the good crystal or the china yet. We're making do with our everyday dishes and jelly glasses."

"That will be fine," Frances said. He took the tea from her hand as she tried to set it before him, letting his fingertips linger on hers as long as possible. He sipped it daintily and made an awful face. "Oh my, this is entirely too sweet and strong. Please don't be offended but I'll have to pour half of it down the drain and add water. I like my tea barely colored and with very little sugar."

"Be my guest. To each his own. We like it black as coffee and with lots of sugar. Southern style," she smiled.

He stood as close to her as he could while he carefully remade his tea and she tore endive greens into a bowl for salad. "What is that lovely perfume you are wearing? It reminds me of gardenias on a hot summer day. I can shut my eyes and see an old plantation home painted a rich dark green with a porch swing. Mimosa trees all abloom and gardenias blooming in the yard."

"It's something the girls gave me for Mother's Day. I think they bought it at Wal–Mart. It's a knock off of some fancy perfume they couldn't afford. I call it Fake Red. The bottle says it's Scarlet. Strange, I never thought of it smelling like gardenias," she almost laughed. Gardenias made her think of fear and tornadoes. At her junior high graduation, her boyfriend brought her a corsage with a beautiful gardenia spread out in the middle of ribbons and bows. Right before the graduation ceremonies, a tornado blew through Nocona. She, along with everyone else in the school at the time, were crowded into the hallway until it passed. She'd never wear anything that reminded her of that night.

"Well, it's most wonderful. You should wear it all the time. Ah, this is just perfect," he held up his glass and looked at her through the pale amber liquid.

Nothing more than murdered water, Mary Jane's grandmother would have said.

"So dear, are you working on another romance book?" He claimed his throne at the head of the table. "I'm sure in the past eleven years you've amassed quite a fortune with your thirty sales. When are you planning to stop writing and do something more spiritually profitable with your time?"

He'd done his own amount of research if he knew how long and how many. *Perhaps the girls are right in their assumption that he expects more out of Paradise than a spinach lasagna*, Mary Jane mused to herself.

"I don't ever intend to stop writing. I hope I've just finished a novel and written 'The End' on the last page when I keel over with a heart attack." She tore the lettuce leaves slowly. Anything to make the job last longer so she didn't have to sit at the table with him.

"Oh, that's just because you have no one in your life to bring you happiness and joy of heart," he said with a sly wink. "Unless of course, that handyman you have living here is more than just hired help. In which case, I would feel honor bound since I am your pastor, if only for one Sunday, to counsel you against such, what with seven little girls looking to you for a role model and guidance."

"Pastor McSwain," she faced him from across the room, ignoring the lettuce totally.

"Please call me Frances. My mother thought that a grand old name when she gave it to me and refused to let anyone call me Frank or Frankie. She was my inspiration to go into the ministry. A wonderful woman. I still live with her over in Saint Jo. I'm only preaching one day at the Spanish Fort church. The new preacher will arrive this week. He's a family man with three little children. He's being moved here from San Antonio to work somewhere down around Nocona. Actually, I'm not a preacher full-time anymore. I just take on little area jobs like this to keep Mother happy. She's up in her eighties now and can't get out on Sunday morning to listen to me preach, but I tape my sermons and take them home to her. We listen to them together on Sunday night then have a nice little supper together. My sister comes in on Sunday morning and fixes her lunch. She would just love this place. Really, I must bring her to see it sometime," he said.

"Frances, it is then, Joe Clay Carter was a highschool classmate of mine. What he does or doesn't do, or how he fits in or doesn't fit into my family, is really none of your business. I just wanted to get that straight right now. I'm a divorced woman with seven little girls and I'm quite aware of my role in their lives," she said icily.

"Forgive me if I offended you," he smiled benevolently. *So she has a bit of spit and sass in her, does she?* That could be taken care of with the proper amount of time. Why, his dear mother could cut through that in no time, as well as have those seven girls toeing the line. And she'd be so comfortable in the downstairs bedroom where Joe Clay had taken up temporary residence. He'd wait a while before he convinced her that the Paradise was the past and Whispering Pines was the future.

"No offense. Just stating facts," she said. *Lord, let him eat fast and get the hell out of my house*, she prayed.

By the time she called the girls down for lunch, she had no appetite. They all paraded in, not a one of them changed into shorts, and still wearing their Sunday school dresses. Endora smiled sweetly at the preacher and patted his hand when she took her place beside him. At that moment, Mary Jane wished she'd given them permission to be on their worst behavior. She wished she'd told them to burp and talk with food in their mouths, and tell him all about how Rae had vomited all over the bed last week and it looked just like his spinach lasagna.

"Frances, will you say grace for us?" Mary Jane set the salad in the middle of the table and took her place, bowing her head to ask forgiveness for her wicked thoughts.

"Of course," Frances beamed.

The cheese on the top of the lasagna is going to be curdled by the time he finishes, Mary Jane thought, opening one eye a slit to see how the girls were taking the five minute blessing slash sermon in disguise. Every one of them had their hands folded in their laps and their heads bowed like perfect angels.

When the amen was finally said and dishes passed, Endora sent the spinach lasagna on down the line and helped herself to the meat dish. "I think I need a lot of energy today. After we eat, I'm going to jump on the trampoline and holler until I don't have a voice. Would you like to jump with me?" She asked the pastor.

"Oh, no, my dear. I'm much too old to be jumping on a trampoline," he chuckled. "This lasagna is delicious. My compliments to the chef. Would it be too presumptuous of me to ask for a portion to take home for my dear mommy's supper? She would so enjoy it. I could bring your plate back tomorrow."

"Oh, we got lots of paper plates," Ursula told him. "We'll be glad to fix up your mother a supper. How about chocolate cake, too? Momma made one yesterday. It's Joe Clay's favorite. Called a Texas Sheet Cake. But he can't be here today. He owns some rental property and he's off seeing about it."

Mary Jane had the urge to shoot her "one of those looks" that would shut her up about Joe Clay but it stopped midair.

"He does love his chocolate. Why he could probably eat half that cake without blinking an eye," she murmured, smiling at Ursula.

"Chocolate and sugar," Frances shuddered. "Oh, no. My dear, no. My mother, nor I, would think of partaking of sugar. It's bad for the body, you know. You children should be eating fresh fruit. Oatmeal for breakfast with only a little butter and milk."

"No butter and brown sugar or maple syrup and lots of cream?" Luna asked, aghast at the idea.

"My, my, I can see you do need training in how to keep your bodies fit," he chuckled. "I'll have to teach you. The first thing you'll sacrifice is sugar of any kind. Only a little bit in your tea. Like this, see? Half of it poured out and water added. And that only on Sunday. Other days, nothing but water. No soda pop. No tea. No coffee. Just good old water. Then you give up meat of any kind. Dairy is fine but only skimmed milk and that in small portions. You'll feel so much better."

"Would you pass that meat lasagna, please, sir? I think I'll have another chunk of it and Momma, we do get to eat the chocolate cake don't we? Or do we have to wait for Joe Clay to come home?" Endora said.

"You can have cake if you finish everything on your plate

so you'd better go easy on that second helping of lasagna, Endora," Mary Jane could have kissed the child.

"Well, praise the lord," Ophelia threw a hand up.

"Tut, tut," Frances clucked. "We shall not take the lord's name in vain."

"I wasn't, Mr. Frances. I promise. I was honestly giving him glory for chocolate cake," Ophelia dropped her eyes contritely and squeezed Ursula's leg under the table.

"You'll have to forgive my sister," Ursula told him. "She's grooming to be a nun."

"Oh, dear, are you Catholic?" He almost choked.

"My stepmother is and I've been thinkin' on it," Ophelia shoveled the last of her salad into her mouth, but she didn't look up. "Seems like it might exorcise the Paradise of all the past if a nun came out of the place, doesn't it?"

Frances sputtered, speechless as he downed half his glass of tea.

"And your father?" He finally asked Ophelia. "Is he Catholic?"

"Oh, we all have different daddies," Luna piped up at that time. "That is, all but me and Endora and that's because we're twins. Rae and Bo have the same daddy 'cause they're twins, too. But the rest of them all have different ones. I don't think my daddy is Catholic and I'm not too sure about my stepmother, Caitlin. She might be. Besides, how old are you if you're too old to jump on a trampoline? Momma is thirty-eight and she still jumps with us."

"I will be forty years old next month," he said slowly. "So you've been married five times?" He looked down his nose, down the long table at Mary Jane.

"Oh, no, I was only married once. To Martin while we were in college. I put him through medical school and then we divorced four years ago," she said.

"That's my daddy," Ursula said, about to begin her story of how they all had different daddies but the same father. The same one she'd told Joe Clay almost a month ago. But she only got out three words when she felt her mother's bare toe kick her shin under the table.

"I see," Frances nodded, the future of Whispering Pines going up in smoke. Mommy might forgive the woman of one divorce. After all, it was most likely her husband's fault. He'd heard through the grapevine that the man was now married to a multi–billionaire and they traveled over the whole world, coming back to Texas only at Christmas. But to forgive her for what had to be multiple affairs; even he wasn't prepared to do that. The yard would have to stay a barren mess and Paradise just might be the right name for the place for a harlot like M.J. Marsh after all.

"After dinner, you can come and pet my kittens," Bo said. "There's five of them and the momma cat. She's a nice old momma cat and don't even mind if you pet the kittens. But you can't hold them because she'll move them off some-where dark and the coyotes might eat them."

"Oh, my dear, I couldn't pet your kittens. Mommy and I are highly allergic to cats. They make our eyes water and sting," Frances said, finishing off the last of his salad and carefully placing his napkin to the side of his plate. "I'm so sorry to eat and run but I really must. Mommy will be expecting me. No, please don't bother yourself to walk me to the door. I suppose the new preacher will be here by next Sunday when the church meets here in Spanish Fort. I've heard that they're considering having services every Sunday. It's not a fact yet but it could happen. Thank you for a lovely meal and for such lively conversation. Good day to you ladies."

When they heard the pickup roar out of the front yard,

Endora looked up from the end of the table and quite angelically said, "Oh, my dear, he has done forgot to take his mommy some lasagna. Don't worry, Momma, I'll see what damage I can do to it for supper."

And that's when all eight broke into a fit of giggles.

And that's when Joe Clay Carter walked into the kitchen.

"What is so funny?" He asked, the chill of his voice causing complete silence.

"You had to have been here," Mary Jane told him.

"My rent house. My family home burned to the ground," he said bluntly.

"I'm so sorry," Mary Jane said. "Have you had lunch?"

"No and I'm starved," he took his place at the end of the table, gave the empty plate and napkin a puzzled look, and looked down the table at the girls. "Who's been sitting in my place?" He asked.

"The preacher man, Frances McSwain, came to dinner. But he's too old to jump on the trampoline. I asked him if he'd like to play on it, but he said he was too old," Luna said.

"He doesn't eat anything that had a face, but I did today. But I'm not going to eat it at supper. I'm going to eat the spinach lasagna," Endora said.

"Why did he come to dinner?" Joe Clay motioned for Mary Jane to sit back down when she hopped up to get him a clean plate. "I can take care of it."

"Because he's interested in Momma. He wants to change the Paradise to Whispering Pecans and he wants to make a flower bed in the front yard with some kind of thing called the climateeitis flower. I think he's going to come back next week but he's not going to preach at the church anymore. We got a new preacher coming. One who has kids," Ursula told him.

"And he doesn't have kids?" Joe Clay helped himself to a

healthy portion of lasagna. "Everyone finished with this?" He pointed toward the big salad bowl.

Eight heads nodded.

"Then I'll just finish it up out of the bowl." He poured ranch dressing on what was left.

"No, he doesn't have kids, and it seems like he liked us all right. He's going to teach us all about how to eat right and his mother might come to see us sometime," Ophelia said.

First his house burned to the ground. Now he'd come home to find that Mary Jane was interested in the preacher. He filled his mouth with lasagna and wanted to kick something. Anything. Even a steel barn door would be all right. He had barely swallowed when his cell phone rang. He reached inside the pocket of his t-shirt and took it out, answering it right at the table.

"Hello," he said, expecting it to be his renter or Pete, telling him the fires had ignited again or some other catastrophic news.

"Joseph Clayton Carter," a familiar voice said in his ear.

"Yes, sir," he almost stopped breathing.

"You know who this is?"

"Yes, I do," he said.

"There's a problem in Central America. A troop is training even as we are speaking. I need a leader. We're going in January first. Can I count on you?"

"I'm retired, sir," Joe Clay said.

"I know that and you can stay retired. I'm not asking you to reenlist, Carter. I'm asking for a week of your time at a salary that would choke a Texas longhorn," he said.

"Is this going to happen often?" Joe Clay asked.

"Probably if you take it, about three or four times a year. We need you to oversee some dangerous missions. Freelance for us, Carter. I'm asking as a favor."

"You can count on me," Joe Clay said. "D.C.?"

"You know what office and how to get in. I'll see you at five o'clock January first."

"January first. Five o'clock. I'll be there," he said and hung up the phone. Fate had just shown him the way out of Montague County, Texas.

Chapter Eight

Joe Clay's lips fascinated Mary Jane. The dip in the center of the top one, the slight outward curve of the bottom one, an almost pout without one feminine trait. Totally masculine. Something in the pit of her stomach churned. She recognized it as desire and tried to push it away but it didn't work.

She couldn't expect to see a man as sexy as Joe Clay Carter every single day and not respond to him, now could she? She tried to reason with herself as they shared the porch swing that Sunday afternoon. If the foot of silent space between them could be filled with words to describe what they both felt right then she wondered what they would be? On his part: disappointment. Bewilderment. Exhaustion. Determination.

Disappointment because he'd just seen his family home burn to the ground. A vision of the house in Nocona where Mary Jane had grown up materialized in Mary Jane's imagination. A two story not far from the school. Her parents brought her home from the hospital as a newborn baby to that house. Then five years ago they'd sold it, bought a motor home, and toured the whole United States, decided they liked Louisiana better than any other place and bought a small house there.

Bewilderment. He'd told someone on the phone during lunch he'd be there on January *first*. She wondered what that was all about. Not that it was a bit of her business. He'd only agreed to work for her until Christmas. She let her gaze go back to those lips and how she wanted to kiss away the disappointment and bewilderment. Slide across the tension filled space between them and taste those lips one more time. See if the episode in the garage was a fluke or if his kisses could haunt her dreams all night long.

Exhaustion. Well, he'd worked all week and then from the looks of him when he came back to Paradise, he'd spent his Sunday morning helping the firemen and/or sorting through what was left of his past. She could rub his shoulders, digging her finger tips into the muscles showing through the t-shirt. She could massage his neck until the tension subsided, but not without kissing those lips when she finished. One little prize for all her hardwork.

Determination. To get the job done so he could leave Paradise and do whatever that phone call entailed. She couldn't blame him. No man wanted a woman with as much baggage as what came with Mary Jane Marsh Simmons. A writing career she had no intentions of stopping. Seven daughters. Six cats out in the utility room. A house that had been a bordello. Not exactly paradise for a man like Joe Clay. More like a prison with rolls and rolls of razor wire on top of a twenty foot fence.

"Was anything salvageable?" She asked, keeping her eyes from his mouth. When he spoke and his lips moved, she'd think of the way they moved so expertly on hers. Not looking didn't help much, though.

"Nothing. I hired a cleanup crew. Pete knew someone. Said it wouldn't take more than half a day. Fire pretty much ate it all," he said.

"I know I said I was sorry, Joe, and I mean it. I really am," she told him.

"I know," he absentmindedly patted her hand.

Lord, just his touch had her wishing she had as much nerve as the heroines in her books. Not a one of them would have thought twice about claiming Joe Clay for their own. Not even her newest one. Miss Sarah, who'd set out to win the sheriff's heart and by golly if by the end of the book she wouldn't have him on his knees, thinking the madam of a bordello was just what he'd always wanted.

"You ever miss Nocona, Texas? All those years when you were in service, only coming home on leave? You ever think about what your life would have been like if you'd stayed in the area? Maybe gone to school and studied to be an architect or taken up the reconstruction business when your dad retired?" She asked.

"Sure I missed it. It was home. And yes, I thought about the what ifs, Mary Jane, but you kind of shot those all down for me right at the end of our senior year," he stopped the swing.

Dead still. Not even a breeze between the Gulf of Mexico and the Nebraska state line. Tension so thick she could scarcely breathe in the hot afternoon air. She hadn't shot down anything for Joe Clay Carter. Not Mary Jane.

"Want to explain that?" she asked.

"Sure, I've just been waiting twenty years to explain it to you," he said, a chill chasing away every bit of warmth in the whole of Montague County.

Mary Jane wouldn't have been surprised for the weather report to include a snow storm right there in the middle of September. A freak thing brought on by the tone of Joe's voice.

"You see, I didn't ask you to the prom so you'd be a stand-in girl for Joyce Brandley. I'd started going with her right after Christmas, trying to make you jealous. I'd had a crush on you from the time we were in the fifth grade, but you never even looked my way. I figured it was because of my scar. Then there we were, seniors in high school. Everything about to change. You planning to go to Baylor and I was looking at it, too. Just so I could be close to you," he paused.

"Joe, I didn't know. I was so plain in school. So much taller than all the other girls. So thin back then. I never thought the big stud football player would really be interested in me. At first when you asked me to the prom, I figured it was a joke. You know, you and the other boys betting on whether you'd ask the plainest girl in high school or not. Then Betsy said it was because you figured I wouldn't refuse and you'd at least show Joyce that you didn't have to go alone. Why weren't you honest with me?" She asked.

"Hey, I was a high school senior with a scar on his face and I got so tongue-tied around you, it was all I could do to get out two sentences asking you to the prom. I'd broken up with Joyce because I wanted to give it one last ditch effort. It took every bit of nerves I had just to ask you. Do you honestly think I could have stood there and told you I'd been in love with you since grade school? So yes, I wonder what our lives might have been if you'd said yes and I'd had an enchanted evening with you. Would it have changed things? Would we have ended up at Baylor together?" He asked.

"But we were kids and that was twenty years ago," she said.

"Yes, we were. Kids on the brink of adulthood who had

no idea what one invitation and one refusal would do to their lives. The stars didn't cross for us, Mary Jane. We missed our chance, didn't we?"

"I suppose we did," she nodded.

He didn't tell her that every woman he'd dated in those twenty years hadn't come up to the mark when he measured her against Mary Jane Marsh. Or that he'd thought he was seeing an apparition that morning she knocked on his motel door. Surely she had to be a maid who looked somewhat like the woman he'd been in love with all those years. Mary Jane wouldn't be knocking on his door.

He didn't mention that he loved living in the house with her, pretending at times that she and that pack of girls were his. Nor that he dreaded Christmas because it would all be over.

"So did you ever think about what would have happened differently in your life if you'd stayed in Nocona?" He asked.

"Of course," she looked at him, or rather at his lips again. How could he have ever thought she was put off by his scar? It only served to make him more ruggedly handsome. "If I'd come back to Nocona to teach English that first year, would my parents have kept our family home? If there had been a chance they would have had one child who would want to live in it, would they have been so quick to sell it? If I'd come back, would I have met you on leave? It's all a bunch of surmising and supposition, though, isn't it? I took the job in Dallas and met Martin. You went into the service and two different people sit here today on the porch of the Paradise," she said.

"You're right. Oh, and that phone call at the dinner table," he inhaled deeply.

"That's your business, Joe Clay. None of mine," she said.

She didn't want to think about him being gone right after Christmas. She sure didn't want to talk about it.

He ignored her. "It was my general. There's a situation in Central America. That's all I know, but I'm to be in D.C. on January first. They'll brief me and I'll take a crew in undercover to do a job. He tells me the pay is good. I don't have to come out of retirement. I'll be working as a hired gun, so to speak. He says he might call several times a year."

"Joe Clay, that's dangerous. You are retired. Leave it at that. Call him back and tell him no. You are too young to risk your life, no matter what the cost," she blanched, all the color leaving her face and fear filling her green eyes.

"There are boys defending our right to sit on this porch right now, Mary Jane. They're not even old enough to buy beer in most states. They're not old enough to register to vote. But they've got a rifle and their orders. They risk their lives everyday and their paycheck for the whole year probably won't be a third of what the one will be for my week's work," he said.

"Your initials stand for Joseph Clay not Jesus Christ, so don't preach at me," she said icily. "I know what goes on in the world. I don't need you to talk down to me."

"I'm leaving now. I'm going to take a nap," he said.

"Don't you run away from me when we're fighting," she jumped up and stood in front of the door. "If you'd told me how you felt back in high school instead of running off to the service, things might have been different. They might not have been. We probably wouldn't have liked each other one bit when we got into a relationship. But you let your fears stop anything that could have been."

"We're not fighting," he said. "I was baring my soul to you, telling you things I've never spoken aloud. But like you said, lady, twenty years is a long time and we're two different people." He scooped her up in his arms as if he was about to carry her over the threshold, turned abruptly around, and set her back down in the swing. "I'm sleepy and this is going to be a long week, so I'm taking a nap. If I'm not awake at supper, don't wake me."

"Damn it!" Mary Jane cursed under her breath. Men! He'd unloaded a bomb on her soul, blowing her past apart, giving her a glimpse of what life might have been if only she'd been brave enough to go to the prom with him. So why did fate and destiny join forces at this time in her life to open up the "what ifs" in her heart and soul? It was possibly the most unfair thing that had ever happened.

She hoped dreams haunted his nap. That every time he shut his eyes he saw her in the garage and felt her lips on his. But then, why would he? Just because the kiss defied gravity and left her floating six feet above the earth didn't mean it had done the same for him. He'd been everywhere in the past twenty years. Exotic ports with equally fascinating women. Females from every walk of life, quite eager to fall into the arms of a big, strong man with a wicked grin, sinfully sexy lips, and a body out of a fitness magazine. Not to mention his abilities to fix anything, repair anything, organize, supervise more than one crew. Why he wasn't married was a complete mystery.

Joe Clay opened a Trace Atkins CD and carefully placed it in his portable player, fitting the expensive headphones over his ears. He didn't want to hear the girls' giggles and screams float across the yard and defy all science as they made their way right through the window panes to his ears. He didn't want to hear a knock on the door if Mary Jane wasn't finished with the fight. He just wanted to fall asleep with Trace singing to him.

It didn't work.

The country singer sang about a father wishing his kids would hurry and grow up and the emptiness when they do. Paradise would be empty without the seven imps who could make him angry and laugh at the same time.

Then he sang about love not supposed to make sense. Well, that was the absolute truth. One hundred percent truth in a three and a half minute song. If it had made sense he and Mary Jane would have explored the "what ifs" way back when. When Trace began to tell in song about how he couldn't swear that he'd be in his woman's life for the rest of her life but he could swear he could love her for the rest of his life, Joe Clay nodded, keeping time with his fingers.

Yes, he'd loved her since fifth grade. Twenty years of women hadn't erased that love and it would go on. That was a given. But it would have to be bittersweet, because any fool could look at the situation in Paradise and see that it wouldn't work. Mary Jane hadn't spent her whole life measuring all the men against Joe Clay.

The next song was about chrome being some girl's favorite color. He wondered what Mary Jane's favorite color was. Red? Was that why she'd wanted to paint the house that horrible shade? Thank goodness she'd changed her mind and decided to give it a nice white look. Mossy green? Like her eyes. Could that be her favorite color? She wore a lot of green when she wasn't running around in cut-off jean shorts and an oversized shirt. Of course, he thought she was as beautiful in the shorts and shirt as the expensive green dress she'd been wearing at the dinner table. Legs. Lord, that woman had legs that went on forever. Long, lean and trim legs that should model low-slung jeans and shorts for some fashion magazine.

The song ended and the haunting sound of fiddles filled

his ears. He could imagine holding Mary Jane in his arms and two stepping around the floor of a dance floor. They'd look good together; her chin right under his. Her body molded to his. One hand with hers tucked inside his thumb; the other holding his Stetson at the small of her back.

Trace was singing about rolling out of Dallas and chasing a dream when Joe Clay shut his eyes. Trace sang about a girl in Texas lighting up the night and being a lonely man but he was leaving there alone. Well, that was a given. Joe Clay would be leaving alone probably a few days before Christmas. The whole Marsh family would be arriving and there wouldn't be a place for Joe Clay in amongst a family. Besides if there were cousins aplenty and holiday fan fare, Endora wouldn't even miss him.

He fell asleep to the singer leaving every light in the house on so she'd know how much he missed her. Joe Clay's last thought before he fell asleep was that if leaving lights on could convince Mary Jane how much he wanted her, Paradise would make the Griswolds' place look dark and dreary.

Mary Jane stomped into the house and deliberately thundered up the stairs, hoping that her footsteps kept him awake. He didn't deserve to sleep when she was wide awake and angry enough to tear up an army tank with a feather.

She grabbed the first CD on the top of the stack and slipped it into the stereo system beside her bed. She spread three journals out before her and opened her chapter book. While the girls played, read, or spent their afternoon however they wanted, she'd get a jump on the next few days' work. She'd gotten first rate insight into the head of her hero anyway. He was half-saint and the other half pure Joe Clay Carter, so he had a stubborn streak that her heroine would hate.

One of her favorite groups began to sing—Highway 101, back when Paulette Carlson was still the lead female singer for them. The lady asked her ex if he'd told his new love that she was sleeping in the bed he'd made for her, and wondered if the pillow she slept on brought her sweet dreams. Mary Jane wished Caitlin anything but sweet dreams. If she hadn't flitted through Martin's life at the height of his mid–life crisis, he might have weathered through the storm. But when a twenty-something woman with more money than Fort Knox beckoned, Martin went. Mary Jane hoped Martin would have to go to the drug store for some of those expensive little pills to keep Miss Bimbo Queen happy.

Mary Jane smiled at that idea. She shouldn't still be harboring resentment. Good grief, it had been four years. She'd gotten on with her life. Written several more bestsellers, been recognized at Romance Writers of America conferences. When she decorated her new office space, the walls would be covered with awards. She'd spent four wonderful years with her girls; years Martin had snatched away from him because Caitlin literally hated kids.

"I've had the best of the two worlds. Proving once and for all that money isn't everything," she said aloud as Paulette sang about a man being someone else's trouble now. That the little stream would be a raging river when the tears came down. Mary Jane had weathered that storm. She'd cried and cried, but unlike the song, she wasn't going to love Martin until the day she died. No sir. That love had died and for the most part the anger was gone. At least most of the time.

She listened to Paulette singing about some woman believing in a fellow's honky tonk heart and not playing second fiddle to the beat of a honky tonk heart. Was that what she would have done if she and Joe Clay had gotten together? If a relationship had been born out of a senior class prom? Would he have still gone to the service and expected her to stay home alone while he went to save the world? To carry a rifle before he could even vote? He didn't like kids, he'd said. Would he have wanted her to follow him around the world and never have a child?

The questions had no answers. She picked up her chapter book and began to write, fast and furious. Her hand cramped. She threw the pen down and shook the pain from her fingers, picked it up again and kept writing. After a while, she threw herself back on the pillows, shut her eyes and literally saw the scene she'd just written play out before her eyes. The madam of Paradise stood on the porch and watched the sheriff ride away on his big black horse after a colossal argument. Someday she'd do that. Stand on the porch and watch Joe Clay ride away in his big black pickup truck. The only difference was that Miss Sarah controlled that sheriff. She would never control Joe Clay Carter.

She was just suffering from a case of raging hormones. She had a right, after four years of loneliness, for her hormones to kick into overdrive. Add the year before that when Martin was seeing Caitlin on the sly and sleeping on the couch more than he slept in her bed and that was a lot of months for the old hormones to hibernate. If they raged, it was long past due.

The only thing she hated was that they'd chosen Joe Clay and his one kiss to jump start them into third gear. Not that she would have wanted Frances to throw the switch on them. Not in this lifetime or the next one either. That man was poison in a clergyman's robe. She could easily see why he hadn't had a wife in his near forty years. But now, Joe Clay, that was a different matter. He was witty and sexy, besides being handsome with those cutting blue eyes and prematurely gray hair.

She was surprised when she opened her eyes to see that it was after five o'clock. She'd slept more than three hours, without a single dream. There was a god in heaven, after all. She gathered her journals and chapter book into a pile and set them on the night stand, stretched all the way to the top of her five feet ten inches and purred like one of Bo's new kittens. She couldn't remember the last time she'd slept so well. Not since before Ursula was born. Not since the days when she and Martin napped together on a Sunday afternoon when he had finished his homework.

In that moment, she realized she was beginning to put it all to rest. After four years, she finally woke up to find she didn't love Martin anymore and she was ready to let him go and allow him to pursue whatever made him happy. It was time to get on with her own pursuit of happiness.

The idea was heady and intoxicating. She looked at the woman in the mirror. Crow's feet around her eyes. No naiveté hiding behind those green eyes. She'd lived long enough to know life wasn't perfect and guarantees weren't promised. But she'd also lived long enough to realize life was only what she made it. No one else was going to grab the bull by the horns, stare him right in the eyes, dare him to a challenge and then hog tie him and brand him if he did.

"Enough philosophizin'," she told the woman in the mirror with a wicked grin. "No matter what profound discoveries you've uncovered this day, supper still has to be cooked and seven little girls taken care of. Good lord, it's so quiet around here, I wonder if they've all been kidnapped."

"Girls, where are you?" She yelled from the top of the steps.

Nothing but silence answered her. Cold tremors shook her body. She'd teased about kidnapping, but suddenly the reality of sleeping so soundly hit her. Where were her children?

"Girls?" She yelled again, an edge to her voice.

The only thing that answered was the mother cat, who ran up the steps to rub around her ankles. She pushed it aside and took the stairs two at a time, rushing out on the front porch just in time to see Joe Clay, all seven girls hopping around him, coming across the pasture beside the house.

She almost wept with relief as she sunk into the porch swing.

"Hey, Momma, guess what? We looked over every inch of this property. Joe Clay showed us the lines. And there's enough room for a horse so I'm asking Daddy to get me one for Christmas," Ophelia said.

"A horse is a big responsibility and we'll talk about it later," Mary Jane said seriously. "For now, we'd better get inside and put some supper on the table."

"And afterwards Joe Clay said if you said it was all right, we could all go into town for banana splits at the Dairy Queen," Endora said, her hand still firmly in Joe Clay's. "He said he'd take us and show us where his house burned down. I want to see what a house looks like all burned down. How does a fire make it nothing but ashes?"

She left Joe Clay explaining the theory of fire and ashes to her youngest twins while the rest of them went inside to heat up leftover lasagna. Had it only been a few hours since the preacher sat at lunch with them? Mercy, it seemed a lifetime ago when he thought she'd had kids by five different men.

"So what were you and Joe Clay fighting about out on the swing?" Ursula asked as she set the table.

"We weren't fighting. We were discussing," Mary Jane prepared a fresh salad and a loaf of store-bought French bread to go with their leftover lasagna.

"You were fighting. Joe Clay said he had been in love with you since fifth grade," Tertia said.

"You were eavesdropping?" Mary Jane spun around, her face hot with a sudden blush. "Where were you?"

. "Hiding in the mimosa tree," Tertia said with a shrug. "And you talked about how things might have been different if you hadn't been so stubborn and would've gone to the prom with him."

"Well, I'll have to remember to check the mimosa tree before I say anything else," Mary Jane snapped.

"Oh, don't be mad at us," Bo said. "We just want what's best for you, Momma. We want you to be happy. You know like Daddy is with Caitlin. She's not a mommy, and I sure wouldn't want to spend more than one day with her. But Daddy loves her. And we want someone to love you like that. We kind of like Joe Clay but if you don't want to go to a prom with him, that's okay. What is a prom, Momma?"

"It's a party that high school kids go to," Joe Clay said from the doorway. He filled it up with his more than six foot frame just like he'd done in the motel room. "I don't think you have to worry about it for a long time. But now, Ursula, she'll most likely start thinking about it before many more years. Looking at books with fancy dresses and dreaming about some Prince Charming coming along in his white pickup truck to take her to the prom at Prairie Grove."

"You going to go with someone in a pickup truck?" Ophelia nudged her sister. "I'd have thought you'd would at least demand a Porsche convertible."

"In Prairie Grove? I'll be lucky if he comes to get me in a white pickup truck instead of a beat up old red one," Ursula giggled.

"What are you going to do when us girls get old enough to date?" Endora asked Joe Clay. "You going to make the boy come in the house and meet the family or can he honk and we get to run down the steps like in the CMT video?"

That drew him up short and an ache squeezed the life out of his heart. The girls started an argument about which CMT video they'd seen that scene in, where the girl ran out of the house and jumped into the car with her boyfriend. Mary Jane didn't appear to even hear them. But Joe Clay would be gone in December. He wouldn't be there to see them leave on their first dates, to have his picture made with them in their prom finery.

And it hurt.

Chapter Nine

A blue norther ushered in October to north central Texas. Temperatures dropped down into the forties. The girls had to hustle around to find jackets and long jeans to wear to school that morning. Joe Clay teased them about turning on the heat in the morning and the air conditioner by mid-afternoon. When they were on the bus, he went to Bo and Rae's room to work and Mary Jane disappeared into her office.

The first Paradise book was on the downhill slope, speedily sliding in toward the finish line. Her editor was ecstatic about the book. As soon as she completed it, she'd finish *The Reckless Knight* and then go right into a story about Lil, one of the girls who had worked at Paradise. For the next two or three years she'd be tied up with the series, and a movie contract already waited in the wings. She wished her personal life was as exciting as her professional one.

After the weekend of the kiss, Joe Clay's house burning, and the phone call, they'd been coolly distant with each other. The girls were the glue that held the whole working relationship together, keeping them entertained at breakfast and supper. The rest of the day they scarcely spoke and then only if it pertained to reconstruction.

Mary Jane flipped a switch, turning on her computer, and sat down to write. She popped a Floyd Cramer disk into the CD player and shut her eyes as the country tinkle of the piano swept through her soul, wiping all other thoughts away. She concentrated on the music, then set her fingers on the keys and the words flowed. The characters in the book began to breathe, live, cry, laugh, work; they became three dimensional. She simply used her ability to work the keyboard and bring them to life.

Until there was a loud knock on the front door. She waited a moment, hearing strained to see if Joe Clay would put aside his tools and go to the door. That's the way it always worked. He took care of the plumbers, the painters, everyone, because that's who always knocked on the door, and he was the one they needed to talk to every time. On the second knock she turned off the CD player and pushed her chair back. Evidently he'd taken one of those boards out to the garage to work his magic on it out there.

Mary Jane swung open the front door to find a short woman on the other side.

"Mary Jane Marsh. I swear you haven't changed a bit," the woman smiled.

"I'm sorry," she shook her head and narrowed her eyes. It was the voice finally that sparked the recognition. "Betsy?" She asked incredulously.

"It's me, darlin'," Betsy Shambles said.

"Come in here. What on earth are you doing in Spanish Fort?" Mary Jane held the screen door open for her old friend and tried to hug her at the same time.

"My oldest is getting married in a few weeks. She wants to have the ceremony here in Montague County, if you can believe it. My mother isn't able to travel, and Suzy wants her grandmother to be at the wedding. So I had to come make arrangements. Glory be, Mary Jane, I could have fainted when Mother told me you'd bought the old Paradise. It looks fabulous, by the way, from the outside. Like some kind of plantation house. And Mother said you were having the whole inside re–done, too," Betsy followed Mary Jane into the kitchen.

"We could take a glass of tea to the living room," Mary Jane looked at the antiquated kitchen.

"Oh, no, girlfriends talk in the kitchen. Put that pitcher of tea right here and sit down, girl. We've got some major catching up to do. For starters, I'll give you the condensed version. Married, like you already know, to Jim right out of high school. He enlisted and we've been everywhere. Had two girls, ten months apart. Decided that they'd have it all even though we were military so I started putting them in these cute little baby contests. After all, that was the way to the Miss America pageant. Then there were the beauty contests. You know how I loved to sew so it just felt natural for me to make those foo-foo dresses for them. Before long I was designing them. Now I run my own company making the things. A Betsy dress is sure to win the contest every time," she smiled.

"Condensed version for me?" Mary Jane sipped her tea.

"I know most of it from the newspapers. Award-winning author. Romances that touch every emotion, according to the reviews. I've got every one of them. Have to admit, with a blush here . . ."

"Betsy, you never blushed in your life. You were the most brazen girl in the whole class and didn't give a royal rat's hind end what anyone thought of you," Mary Jane butted in with a giggle.

"Well, I'm blushing now. I brought every one of your books in my car to have you sign them for me. My girls can scarcely believe that I've got the nerve just to walk up to your porch and knock on the door. They said it didn't matter that we were friends in high school. Twenty years is a long time, and we didn't stay in touch," Betsy said.

"Of course you can knock on my door and of course I'll sign your books. So we didn't stay in touch, we were good friends then and still are. Life just led us down different paths and both of us know how terrible we are about writing or calling. Life got in the way of friendship, didn't it?" Mary Jane said.

"It sure did, but honey it's been a ride. I've loved every minute of it. No laying back waiting for the days to pass for me or you either, evidently. We've grabbed a hold of the rope and rode this old bull the full eight seconds, haven't we? Who'd a thought a designer and a writer both would come out of Nocona?" Betsy poured another glass of tea.

Betsy had been a short, voluptuous girl in high school. Top heavy. Tiny waist. Well-rounded hips. Marilyn Monroe in a shorter form. Blonde hair. Wide mouth. Enough sex appeal to turn all the little boys' heads from the time she was in junior high school. The hair was still blonde. The waist had thickened considerably. The mouth had a few wrinkles around it, but she was still a beauty.

"Who'd a thought it?" Mary Jane nodded.

"Now tell me. You married some doctor down in Dallas. How in the devil did you get him to come to Nocona, Texas? I looked in the phone book and didn't see a new listing with Dr. Simmons. Does he maybe work out of Wichita Falls?" Betsy asked.

"Martin and I married while he was in college. We divorced four years ago, a year after he got a case of early mid–life crisis. He got a twenty-something bimbo queen who has more money than a sultan. I got seven girls and a healthy child support and alimony check. What I wanted were parts of his anatomy put in a jar of vinegar at the time. I've come to grips with it, better since I moved here," Mary Jane answered.

"I'm sorry. But seven girls? Mercy, I thought I'd done something out of the ordinary with two just ten months apart. The oldest is nineteen. Marrying another army brat who is a student in college just like she is. When he's got a degree he'll enlist as a first Louie. Now tell me about those seven girls," Mary Jane leaned forward, ready to listen.

"First one, Ursula, was born when Martin was still in school and I was teaching. Second one, Ophelia, was supposed to be a boy. We decided to try one more time for the boy. We got Tertia, a third daughter. That was it. Martin was already referring to our family as the orphanage. Then the pill failed and we got twin girls out of that deal, Rae and Bo. Martin went in for a vasectomy when they were tiny. Only he didn't see any sense in going back for the follow up. So we got twin girls again, Luna and Endora, age seven now," Mary Jane said.

"Where did you get those names?" Betsy asked. "Do they hate you for laying that on them?"

"No, they all seem to love their individuality. So you got Suzy and who else?" Mary Jane asked.

"Jamie," Betsy said. "Suzy after me. Elizabeth Sue. Jamie after Jim whose real name is James Dean. Mother said you've got a whole crew working out here. I can believe it. Last time I saw this old place was our senior year when we all came out here to see if it was haunted. Remember?"

"Yes, we were into that whole haunted thing, weren't we?" Mary Jane laughed. "I think the Baker Hotel in Mineral Wells was more haunted than Paradise, though."

"Oh Lord, that place gave me the creeps. I swear I could smell perfume in one of the rooms and that noise we all heard. I 'bout had to go find a clean pair of underpants," Betsy laughed with her.

"This is nice. Catching up. Visiting. Let's don't let twenty years get by us again," Mary Jane said.

"Deal. But it'll be easier now. I come home every three months faithful as clockwork to check on Mother. Since the famous M. J. Marsh doesn't throw old friends off her porch, I'll come out to see you," Betsy said.

"Hey, is that the plumber . . ." Joe Clay stopped in the kitchen doorway. "Well, Betsy, it's been a long time."

"Good Lord, Joe Clay Carter, what in the devil are you doing here?" Betsy jumped up and gave him a hug.

"Working, woman. Working," he grinned.

An honest, happy grin. One Mary Jane hadn't seen in weeks. She was so jealous she would have liked to slap it off his face with the blunt end of a shovel.

"You retired out of the service at twenty?" She asked, pulling him back to the table and motioning for him to sit down as she made herself at home and found a glass for him. "Talk to us. It's like a reunion."

Joe Clay caught the freezing look from Mary Jane and pushed the chair back. "Can't. Sorry. Got a room to make princess beautiful with a deadline to get it done. Two of Mary Jane's urchins, Rae and Bo, have me doing double time so they can move in. Good to see you. Tell Jim hello and to come around. He staying in for the thirty?"

"I suppose. He says he's too young to retire at thirty-eight.

Besides he's got a wedding to pay for this year and possibly another one next year," Betsy told him.

"Well, tell him next time he's in town we'll have to work up a poker game," Joe Clay waved over his shoulder and disappeared up the staircase.

"Sweet Jesus, how did you get him to work for you?" Betsy whispered, her eyes glittering.

"I asked him. He was living in a motel. I went down there and made him a deal he couldn't refuse," Mary Jane said.

"Honey, you could have offered him fodder for pay and he would have worked for you just to be near you," Betsy said.

"Oh, come on, Betsy, we're not in high school. We're adults. That sounds like fifth grade talk," Mary Jane said.

"He's been in love with you his whole life," Betsy said. "He and Jim weren't in the same branch of the military. Joe Clay was one of those highly trained professionals," she made quotation marks with her fingers. "Jim is a plain old Sergeant. But they've stayed in touch through the years. When their paths crossed they made time for a beer and a visit. So believe me, I know!"

"Oh, posh, just because he never married doesn't mean he's still in love with that skinny little girl from high school," Mary Jane actually blushed.

"You haven't even been flirting with him? I can tell. He wouldn't sit down and talk to us. You've been giving him the cold shoulder. What's the matter with you, girl? He's handsome, rich, and never married because he can't find anyone to measure up to you," Betsy kept whispering.

"And that's pretty heavy stuff," Mary Jane shook her head. "And now that I think about it, why didn't you tell me he liked me in high school?"

"Because you wouldn't have believed it. Besides back then with your save–the–world attitude, you would have felt honor-bound to go with him to keep from hurting his feelings. Jim and me, well, we figured that would be worse than just turning him down, so we let the whole thing play out the way it would rather than interfering," Betsy told her.

"I see," Mary Jane said. But she didn't. Her whole life might have been altered if she'd known then what she knew now. Of course, it might not have been, either, because who's to say she wouldn't have turned out to be the same woman that Martin fell out of love with. Perhaps, Joe Clay would have had trouble keeping his eyes from going astray, too after seven kids and a mid–life crisis.

"So do you two even talk?" Betsy asked.

"Yes, we discuss the job every day. He has breakfast with the girls and me every morning and supper with us at night. Endora loves him. It'll be hard when he goes away after Christmas," Mary Jane said.

"Where's he going?" Betsy was still whispering.

"I don't know. D.C. Then on some big secret thing to Central America. Says he's going to do some contract labor for the government. Overseeing some covert operations," Mary Jane said.

"Doesn't that scare the liver out of you?" Betsy asked, her voice finally back to normal.

"Why should it? He's going to be finished here by Christmas. That was the deal. There's no happily ever after waiting in the wings. He doesn't like kids. I've got seven. The stars might have crossed for us twenty years ago, but we missed the chance. We're two different people. Two very different people," Mary Jane told her.

"Yes, you are, but you've still got the same heart beating inside your chests. Oh, my, look at the time. That sounded cliché didn't it? But I've really got to go. I told Mother we'd go to the Dairy Queen for lunch today. Her cronies all go there and eat red beans and cornbread once a week, and she wants to go. I'll just leave the books with you and pick them up next month when we come for the wedding. That way you can put something in them that will make my daughters both swoon," Betsy was on her feet and talking the whole way to the front door. "I'll call you next week from California. We'll keep in better touch, I promise."

"Do that, and when the book I'm working on now about Paradise comes out, I'll sign one for each of your daughters, too," Mary Jane said.

"Lord, they'll be in your debt forever. You'll have to bring your tribe to the wedding. I'd love to meet them all," Betsy handed her the box and waved from the car window as she sped down the driveway, leaving a trail of dust in her wake.

Joe Clay heard the car leaving and wandered out into the hallway. He stood at the top of the steps and looked his fill of Mary Jane. Times like this didn't come often and memories would have to sustain him in the long years ahead. Sure, she was a little heavier than she'd been in high school, but like Trace Atkins sang in his song, she was one hot momma. The girl had grown into a fine specimen of a woman. Even more so than he'd imagined all those years when he compared first one woman and then another to her.

She turned abruptly and caught him staring down at her, a soft, sensual look in his eyes that stirred her own heart, breaking chains like they were nothing more than sewing threads. Pulsating looks that brought crimson to her cheeks, burning them with a red hot fire born from her own thoughts. She was foolish to entertain such notions. It was created from the conversation she'd just had with Betsy. Going back to youth. Doing the girlfriend thing around the kitchen table.

"What?" she snapped.

"Nothing," he said just as shortly.

"You going to take time out now for lunch or go back to writing?" he asked. "I'm hungry."

"Me, too," she said honestly. She'd heard her mother say a million times that she knew better than to let her father, Thomas Marsh, ever get hungry. Marsh men got a plumb feral look in their eyes when they were hungry and their women better have something brewing on the stove or they turned mean. Evidently, Joe Clay was cut from the same bolt of cloth as her father. Hunger produced a funny look in the eyes. Not entirely unlike the look of love; but love for food, not woman.

"What'll it be, then?" he asked, dropping a leather carpenter's apron on the wood floor with a loud thump and starting down the stairs toward her. "Peanut butter and marshmallow cream sandwiches? Ham and cheese? Name your poison."

"How about we take an hour and run into Nocona to the Dairy Queen? Betsy said they're serving red beans and corn-bread today. I could use a break and that sure sounds good with the north wind howling," she said. Anything to get them out of the house so she could escape the longing to kiss him again.

"Do I need to change?" He dusted off his jeans with the back of his hand.

"I don't intend to," she picked up a bright orange hooded sweatshirt and jerked it down over her head. The tail end of her red and green plaid shirt hung below the bottom, down over tight blue jeans with frayed cuffs.

"Then let's go see how much damage we can do to the beans and cornbread buffet at the DQ," he said, holding the door for her.

The place was packed by the time they arrived. Betsy and her mother were nowhere in sight, but half of Montague County was there, including friends of Mary Jane's parents who wanted to know where they were and when they'd be coming for a visit now that Mary Jane had come back home where she belonged. Friends of Joe Clay's folks stopped him at nearly every table to express their sympathy over the loss of his family home.

Finally they got through the maze to fill their styrofoam bowls with beans and help themselves to hushpuppies and pickles and find a booth inside the no smoking area decorated with Coca Cola trays, and interesting prints of clowns and the Texas flag. Joe Clay tore three hushpuppies apart and dropped them into his beans.

"Mmmm," he made appreciative noises when he took his first bite.

She did the same at the exact same time.

"Good idea you had there, boss lady," he looked up through the glass window dividing the smoking section from the non smoking. An old man, gray whiskers, blue eyes set in a bed of wrinkles, gave him the thumbs up sign and a broad wink. Joe Clay did not for one minute think that his father's old friend was telling him the beans were wonderful.

"Does taste good, doesn't it? I understand they serve them every Wednesday. We've been missing out on a good thing here, Mr. Carter," she said.

"We've been missing out on a lot of good things, Mrs. Simmons," he said, paralyzing her eyes when she abruptly looked up. "But it's our own stubbornness that makes us do it, so no one can pity us."

"Want to talk a little plainer?" She asked, her heart stopping dead still in her chest.

"No, I don't think I do. Either you understood it or you

didn't. Either you agree or you don't. Right now I'm going to eat all these beans and then go back for more," he said.

"Okay then, I'll just take it anyway I want," she said.

"Why, Mary Jane Marsh and Joe Clay Carter. I heard you two was living together but I told Gracie there wasn't no way. Not Mary Jane. She's got too much sense to be taken in by that good lookin' tall drink of Texas water," Angie Wilson said right at her elbow.

Joe Clay just smiled and kept eating. *Let Mary Jane talk herself out of that one.* Personally he didn't care if the likes of Angie Wilson did think they were living together. It would be just one more woman he didn't have to contend with. She'd married one of his poker buddies a couple of years out of high school, and the poor man had had a devil of a time making enough money to keep her in hair dye and short-tailed skirts.

"I bought the Paradise," Mary Jane stammered, not missing for one minute the long, languishing looks Angie threw in Joe Clay's lap. Not his face. Not his chest, but his lap. Mary Jane had the urge to throw her bowl of beans at the woman.

"That old brothel? You? Lord, that's a laugh. You were the straightest arrow ever to come out of Nocona, Texas. My goodness, girl, what are you going to do with that old place?" Angie pushed herself in beside Joe Clay and dropped her red purse on the floor.

"I hired Joe Clay to remodel it for me. I have seven daughters and it's a nice, big house. Quiet out there where I can get my writing done," Mary Jane said.

"Heard that you were writing. Now that don't surprise me none. You was always bookish and smart. You ever put any steam in your books? No, of course not. Not Mary Jane," Angie giggled at her own idea of what Mary Jane would write. "So Joe Clay, you sure didn't change much 'cept for that gray hair and it's just icing on the cake." She reached under the table and squeezed his thigh.

He picked up her hand and laid it on the table. "You're a married woman, Angie. Thomas is a good man. Put your hands on him; not me."

Angie's laughter sounded like cracking glass. "Ain't you the funny one? Remember when we all drove down to Mineral Wells to that ratty old hotel? You didn't mind me putting my hand on your leg that night."

"Your memory and mine are a might different. Besides, that was twenty years ago. Things change in twenty years," Joe Clay told her.

"You really just her handy dandy fix-it-up man? You're not living with her?" Angie asked.

"That is really none of your business," Mary Jane said bluntly.

"Ah, the mouse has a voice," Angie said.

"The mouse would like you to leave, now. Joe Clay and I were having a discussion," Mary Jane said.

"Well, whatever," Angie threw her stove pipe black hair over her shoulder. "Don't let it be said I'd stick around where I'm not wanted. But don't be trying to pull the wool over my eyes, either, darlin'. If you'd had any sense or nerves you coulda had him in high school, but like we said, twenty years is a long time. You didn't weather well. I'm sure he could do better. Ta-ta, you two. Enjoy your discussion." She slid out of the booth, waved at a woman in a skirt even shorter than hers and made her way across the restaurant, wiggling her hips provocatively to let Joe Clay know what he'd refused.

"Old classmates. Angels or devils?" A big grin lit up his face.

"Guess you got to have both to keep life in perfect balance. She makes a wonderful prototype for a slutty woman trying to steal my sheriff away from the madam of the Paradise," she told him.

"You're writing a story about the Paradise? The girls said you were doing an English historical," he said.

"I was and I am. *A Visit to Paradise* will be finished before Christmas. I'll go back and finish *The Reckless Knight* then. And my editor wants me to do a whole series about what happened to the ladies who worked at the Paradise. Lil is going to be the heroine in the second book. Also, I'll claim a moment of bragging rights here, which isn't my style at all. There have been offers for movie rights to the whole series. Either a movie or a mini–series," she told him, not knowing whether she was sharing the good news with him as her friend, or one-upping Angie and all that cheap sex appeal that oozed from her.

"That's wonderful. And while we're talking about you for a change, let me assure you that what Angie said is pure evil envy. Your hair is as black as she wants hers to be. Your eyes as sexy as she tries to make hers look. And the years have been good to you, Mary Jane. I'm not even comparing you to someone else. Just stating facts. You were a lovely young woman. You're a sensational grownup."

"Flattery will get you a bowl of beans every Wednesday. But they'll be served at home or else I'm going to put out a contract on Angie by next week. I don't think my ego would take a steady dose of her. I'd have to draw back, double up my fist, and do something so unladylike that it would land me in the Nocona jail if I had to deal with her very often. Then Martin would swoop in and take my girls. Caitlin would have an apoplexy. The world would stop turning. All because of one woman who's got a big mouth," she whispered conspiratorially, leaning across the table and keeping one eye cocked toward Angie who was staring blatantly across the room.

"Just as soon eat them at home anyway. Besides she's not

worth the price of the bullet to stop that wicked tongue of hers," Joe Clay drawled. "I'm going back for seconds. Want me to refill your bowl?"

"Think that would constitute us living together?" she asked.

"Never know," he grinned.

She handed him the bowl and winked at Angie.

Chapter Ten

"My old bachelor friend is turning into a family man,"
Jim nudged Joe Clay. "Never thought I'd see that day."

"You still haven't so don't start gloating," Joe Clay held
two paper cones of half-eaten cotton candy while Luna and
Endora rode the ponies at the Halloween festival in Nocona.

"Oh, but I will gloat," Jim chuckled. "I won't be here
when the end credits start rolling so I'll just enjoy my gloating now."

"Has to be a movie before there's end credits," Joe Clay
said. "Before there's a movie, there's script writing. Selling
the script. Talking stars into playing in it. Making the movie.
Old as we are if I started right now today, there might not be
time to get to the end credits."

"Script was written years ago. From the look on your face
around Mary Jane's girls, I'd say the script is sold. Now you
just got to talk those two famous people into playing the
parts. I won't be calling no names but their initials are J.C.
and M.J.," Jim told him.

"The pink one is mine," Endora, dressed as the good

witch in a pink costume with a pointed hat, sparkling in the harsh lights of bare light bulbs, ran from the ponies back to where Jim and Joe Clay waited. "Come on, let's go see what's in that booth over there."

"The purple one is mine," Luna reached out for her cotton candy. She was Endora's opposite. The wicked witch in a black costume with a tall black hat. Somehow she just didn't pull it off as well as Endora. Something about blonde curls and big blue eyes didn't go with a mean witch. "That's the fishing booth. Can we do it, Joe Clay? Will you take me fishing for real before it gets cold? Will you bait the hook for me? I can't stand to touch worms."

"One question at a time," Joe Clay said.

"I'm glad my two are raised," Jim said, watching his friend lick the sticky coating from his hands. "They were fun at that age, but I don't envy you the job ahead of you."

"There is no job ahead of me," Joe Clay said. "Not that I wouldn't like for there to be sometimes, but Mary Jane got burned bad with that first marriage and she's not ready for any kind of relationship. Especially not with an ex–marine who went into the reconstruction job by letting her know up front he didn't like kids."

"Any fool could tell that you love kids. The few times you visited us, you spoiled Suzy and Jamie so bad Betsy said she wasn't ever letting your shadow cross her front door again," Jim watched Luna and Endora run back to the curb where Mary Jane and Betsy sat.

"But not my own. The thought of working with seven girls in the house about sent me packing. Even with the idea of Mary Jane being so close I could see her every day," Joe Clay told him.

"It ain't over until the fat lady sings," Jim said. "And I ain't hearing a single melody floating through the air. Just call me if you see those end credits so I can say 'I told you so' and in case I forget, thanks for tomorrow."

"You're more than welcome but I didn't have a lot to do with it." A grin split Joe Clay's handsome face.

"That's not what I heard and certainly not what I believe. Suzy is ecstatic over the way everything looks. And besides, it saved me a bundle," Jim said.

"That's what single old bachelor friends are for," Joe Clay let Endora and Luna lead him off to the fishing booth.

The Paradise literally looked like something from a fairy princess book. Pink bunting hung from the upstairs balcony. Twinkle lights flickered on and off amongst huge burgundy bows. The front door was an archway with greenery twining up and over the top where a pair of wedding bells really did ring out every time the cool north wind blew. Pink silk roses and illusion made the porch swing into something ethereal.

"Momma, this is the most bestest night of my life," Endora danced around in her mother's bedroom.

"It's going to be the worst night of your life if you don't stand still and let me get your hair fixed," Mary Jane told her youngest.

"Who would have thought this old place would look like this? I mean, the first time we looked at it, it was so ugly and now it's so pretty. Momma, do you think after the wedding, we can go ahead and put up the Christmas lights? It'll be all plain when they take down all the pretty stuff," Endora said.

"No, ma'am," Mary Jane let herself be caught up in the magic of the night. "Remember, in our house we have Thanksgiving. Just us! That's tradition. Then the next day we start Christmas. No buying gifts or decorating before Thanksgiving is over. That's our tradition."

"I know, Momma. But we got this new house and we

could start a new tradition in Paradise, couldn't we?" Endora pleaded.

"Why do you want to do that?" Mary Jane asked.

"Because Joe Clay has been telling us he'll be gone at Christmas. He's already got Rae and Bo's room done and is about to get ours finished. Then he'll do yours and the guest room, and Momma, I want him to see the lights and the house all pretty. Maybe if he sees it all like the Griswolds' he'll stay," Endora begged.

"I figured you'd have an ulterior motive," Mary Jane gave Endora's hair a light coat of hair spray. At that it would probably look like she'd ran halfway across the county in a blowing blue norther by the time they got to the wedding.

"What's that? Did you put motive in my hair? And what's a unterry motive?" Endora asked.

"Ulterior motive is when you've got something else in mind. You've got it in mind to keep Joe Clay here so you want to entice him to stay with the lights," Mary Jane explained.

"Then I guess I got one of them things. You won't make me take that ugly pink medicine for it, will you?" Endora giggled and ran out of the room, her hair already bouncing around.

Mary Jane put the finishing touches on her makeup, pulled her long dark tresses back with a wide silver clip, added a silver chain with a small diamond drop and earrings to match and was ready to go. The simple column dress in burgundy velvet fit her long, slim figure snuggly. She hoped not too tightly. She sure didn't want a reputation like Angie had.

Angie. She moaned aloud. Surely Betsy hadn't invited Angie to the wedding. Lord have mercy and drop down miracles, because if she had to contend with that woman in her house for the whole reception, she might be guilty of homicide before the night was done. Joe Clay might sure enough have the job of burying a body under the mimosa tree, like they'd talked about that morning at the Dairy Queen.

It was an evening of celebration for more than one occasion. Betsy's oldest daughter was getting married and the reception afterwards was being held at the Paradise. When Betsy went looking for a place for the reception, she couldn't find a thing that wasn't already booked. She could use the fellowship hall of her mother's church, but she wanted something cozier. That's when she called Mary Jane. The Paradise had a living room big enough to handle a reception, plus that wonderful bathroom with all those sinks and Suzy could use one of the girls' bedrooms to change into her going–away outfit.

It had been more fun than Mary Jane had had in years. The constant phone calls. The planning. The camaraderie she and Betsy had rekindled after all the years. The florists had arrived two hours ago, setting up candles and decorations. The caterers had commandeered her kitchen early that morning.

The other half of the celebration coin was that she'd mailed the hard copy of *A Visit to Paradise* the day before, sending the final chapters by e–mail to her editor at the same time. Norm called her when he'd read the last words she'd written, thrilled with the whole story. No rewrites. The contract was in the mail. When could he see the first chapters of the book about Lil? She'd reminded him that she still had to finish *The Reckless Knight*. It already had a publication date for the following September. He'd told her to get busy and finish that one so she could focus on the rest of the Paradise series.

"Well, don't you look lovely tonight?" Joe Clay held his hand out to Mary Jane as she descended the stairs.

She took it on the third step from the bottom, only slightly surprised at the way the soft touch of his big, callused hands made her want to fall into his arms. "Thank you, kind sir, and you are not so shabby yourself. I didn't know you owned a tux."

"Well, it's not a real tux. Just a western tuxedo jacket. Can't abide those loose-fitting britches, so I just bought the jacket and every time I'm called upon for a formal affair, I buy a new pair of black jeans. Polished my boots, too. See?" He held up a foot.

"Right nice, Mr. Carter. You get an A for effort, tonight," Mary Jane smiled brightly.

He pulled her hand just enough to send her tumbling into his arms. "I'd like to have an A for something else."

"Mother, it's only thirty minutes until the wedding," Ophelia said from the top of the stairs. "We've got to get Ursula out of the bathroom. She's got a pimple on her chin and it's the end of the world. Paradise is going to be blown apart by meteorites, maybe even from Krypton because she can't be seen outside of the bathroom with a pimple."

"So much for the grading system," Mary Jane pushed away from him. "Ophelia, it's only a couple of years until you'll have pimples, too."

"Oh. My. Goodness," she exclaimed, pressing her hands to her cheeks. "If I become a Baptist nun, will I have them? Surely God wouldn't let a nun get a pimple? Where do they come from anyway?"

"Hormones," Mary Jane said. "And with all your theatrics, you're going to get them in double doses."

"I feel faint but I shall rally around my sister. Momma, does hormones have anything to do with us living in a brothel? Because if it does, maybe we'd better move," Ophelia said.

"Oh, good grief. The wagon train leaves in thirty seconds, with or without pimples," she yelled up to the girls.

A rumble of running footsteps hurried down the steps, stopping in a line at the front door.

"Ursula?" Mary Jane hollered one more time. "Staying or going?"

Holding her head high and her back straight, she descended like royalty.

"That's my girl. A good haughty spirit will keep everyone away and no one will ever see that little tiny red dot on your chin," Mary Jane said.

"Yes, they will, but I can't see it so I'm going to pretend it's not there," Ursula told them. "Besides it's my first one. I wrote it down in my diary so I'll never forget. I got my first pimple when I was thirteen and a half. I bet I got mine before Ophelia gets hers."

Joe Clay chuckled and held the door for the whole bunch of them. Life had never been so sweet. Folks said God always saved the sweetest for the last. Well, Joe Clay figured he was getting pretty near the pearly gates, because it couldn't get much sweeter. Of course, folks said too that all good things must eventually come to an end. So this too would pass. He'd go back to being a lonely bachelor and loving the solitude. Or would he? Of course he would. Mary Jane had never given him one moment's inkling that there was one thing more she wanted from life. She had her writing and her girls. She didn't need an old military freak like Joe Clay added to the mixture.

Betsy had arranged for the ushers to seat Joe Clay, Mary Jane, and the girls on the pew right behind the family. She'd instructed the florists at the church to pin a corsage on Mary Jane and boutonniere on Joe Clay. Each of the girls were to have a wrist corsage.

They took their seats and waited. Mary Jane couldn't remember the last time she'd had a corsage. She stuck her nose into the white roses and inhaled deeply. No scent, but she pretended. Hot house roses seldom put forth the rich aroma of a plain old yard rose. She thought about Frances and his ideas for her lawn. True, he had other ideas that were promptly doused when Ursula began her "we all have different daddies" story but the idea of a lovely yard suddenly appealed to her. Roses to be pampered. And other things that could take the heat without too much work other than what a water hose could provide. Crape myrtles. Petunias. Marigolds. Lantana.

She leaned forward and looked down the pew. Joe Clay was all the way at the other end. How had that happened? Then she remembered. She'd been right beside him and he stepped aside to let her go between the pews, like a good old Texas gentleman. Then the girls had followed her. So there they were, bookcasing seven little girls.

Ursula sat next to her mother. Holding her head up high to defy that tiny little red dot on her chin, she was the rose, Mary Jane decided. The poised one. The sweet-natured child. If Ursula was a beautiful summer pink rose, then Ophelia was a gardenia. Full of life and rich aroma. Ready to live every day to the fullest, without a care that the gardenia blossom was fragile. Tertia was the marigold. Sturdy, dependable. Rae and Bo? They had to be daisies. And Luna and Endora, petunias. Grow anywhere. Wild and brilliant.

What am I? Mary Jane asked herself. Was she a lantana? Not a rose with a lovely odor and graceful petals. But a bit of a stinky flower that bloomed and bloomed in spite of the heat. Something that looked pretty in a garden but was near worthless in a bouquet. No one ever heard of a bride choosing lantana for her bouquet. Maybe that's why Mary Jane would never be a bride again. She was plain old yard-grown lantana.

The music began. Betsy's brother wheeled the grand-mother down the aisle in a wheelchair with illusion bows and white roses decorating it. The mothers were seated. The groom, looking all debonair and handsome in his black tux, along with his brother who served as his best man and the preacher, came from a side room at the front of the church. Then Jamie began her slow stroll down the aisle. She wore a pink satin dress with an off the shoulder ruffled neckline and a bouffant skirt and a wide-brimmed burgundy hat trimmed in pink ribbons and lace. Her bouquet was a fall of pink, white, and burgundy roses.

When she turned to face the congregation, the pianist hit the chords to begin the wedding march. Everyone stood. The back doors swung open and Suzy appeared on Jim's arm. Jim wore his dress uniform, resplendent with a chest full of medals. Suzy was truly a modern day Cinderella. White bil-lowing illusion over double-backed bridal satin. A sweeping skirt that filled the whole aisle. Long chapel length train, monogrammed in exquisite embroidery with the initial B for her new last name. A veil covered her face, allowing only a glimpse of her happiness to shine through in a smile that excluded everyone but the groom.

Joe Clay wondered if he'd be invited to watch the wed-dings of the seven girls in the pew with him that evening. Would they remember him or would he turn into just the man who did the remodeling work on their house that first year they lived there? Would they remember that he'd built the archway in front of the door for this wedding and drag it out of the garage to use again?

"Ain't it pretty?" Endora tugged at his hand and held up her arms. "Hold me so I can see better."

"Me, too," Luna leaned around and whispered.

By the time the preacher had begun the ceremony by asking who was giving the bride into the hands of the groom, Joe Clay had a little blonde-haired girl on each hip.

The wedding lasted less than an hour and then the minister announced that everyone there was invited to the reception which was being held at the Paradise, the home of M. J. Marsh in Spanish Fort.

Mary Jane looked around as the people filed out of the church but she didn't see Angie. She felt relieved and suddenly overjoyed, but the euphoria only lasted until they parked the car at Paradise. Angie was waiting inside the living room, sitting on the sofa, munching on cashews.

"Hey, I missed the wedding but wild horses couldn't keep me away from a reception out here," she said.

"I'd like to turn wild horses loose on her," Mary Jane mumbled.

"Temper. Temper," Joe Clay said, a grin tickling the corners of his mouth. "Besides, here come the rest of the congregation and she'll get lost in it."

"I'm Ursula, Mary Jane's oldest daughter," she introduced herself and extended her hand.

Angie shook hands with her, "I'm Angie, one of Betsy and your mother's old school buddies. My, my, you are a pretty thing. A little bit of makeup and you'd be ready for modeling. Got a boyfriend yet?"

"Can't wear makeup yet, and Momma says I can't date yet either. I'm only thirteen . . . and a half," she said.

"Honey, you come see Angie and I'll show you just how pretty you can be," Angie said.

"Oh . . . ummm . . ." Ursula took one look at Angie with her coarse, dyed black hair, layers of makeup, and short red leather mini-skirt and opened her mouth to respond. The woman had to be the original old girl who'd started up Paradise. Or else it was her ghost.

"Ursula, be nice," Mary Jane murmured so close to her ear that only she heard it.

"Thank you, but I'm pretty happy with the way I am, pimple on my chin and all," Ursula said.

People began to arrive in groups before Ophelia could say another word. Mary Jane checked on the kitchen. Caterers were doing fine without her help. All she had to do was mix and mingle, visit and enjoy the reception.

"So, you weren't let off the hook after all. Dear old Angie did show up," Joe Clay caught her right outside the kitchen door.

"Honey, it's you she was sizing up when we first walked in. She's only here to string barb wire around me. She's here to talk you outside. Notice she did not bring a husband," Mary Jane said.

"I'm not interested in Angie. Never have been," Joe Clay stepped closer, resting a hand on Mary Jane's shoulder.

"Joe Clay?" Ophelia whispered right at his elbow.

How on earth did Mary Jane and her ex-husband ever have those last two sets of twins? he wondered. Every time he got within a second of making a move, one of the kids was there.

"Yes, Ophelia," he whispered back.

"Do you believe in ghosts?" she asked. "Because I think we got one in this house. That woman in our living room. The one that looks like . . . well, like she was the lady who had Paradise built. I think she's a ghost. Or else one of them reincarnated people. The ones who come back again. She ain't real, is she? She's got to be a ghost. Ladies don't go to weddings and fancy receptions looking like that."

Mary Jane's soft giggles erupted into a full-fledged laugh. "Out of the mouths of babes," she said between hiccups.

"You going to answer her?" Joe Clay's chest ached with suppressed laughter.

"She asked you, not me," Mary Jane said.

"Don't matter who answers me. I just want to know if she's real or if she's going to haunt our house. Do we need to call a priest to take her spirit away? I don't want to wake up at night and see her in the hallway. It would scare me out of years and I'd have pimples before my time," Ophelia said seriously.

"She's real. She's not a ghost. She thinks she's beautiful. Don't listen to a word she says and be nice," Mary Jane said.

"Whew," Ophelia wiped her brow. "Now you go on and kiss Momma like you was wanting to do." She ran off back toward the living room.

"Out of the mouths of babes?" Joe Clay looked at Mary Jane.

"I just drop down on my knees every day and give thanks that Ophelia wasn't twins," Mary Jane tried to cut the tension with humor.

"Mary Jane, it's beautiful. Could you help me bustle up my train?" Suzy said. "Uncle Joe Clay, you've come through again. I'll never be able to thank either of you enough."

"Sure, honey, turn around," Mary Jane would someday dedicate a book to Suzy for arriving at just the right moment.

"And you are very welcome. When are you cutting that cake?" Joe Clay wanted to kick the cake like a football out in the front yard. Was there ever going to be a time when he had Mary Jane to himself?

At midnight when the caterers finally had the place cleaned up, when the florists had come to reclaim all the brass candelabra softly lighting every corner, when the wedding cake was nothing but a pile of crumbs, when the bride and groom had driven away in their big shiny black limousine for a honeymoon in Cancun, when Jim and Betsy had thanked them no less than a hundred times, Mary Jane and Joe Clay collapsed on the living room sofa.

"So did you get any ideas for your writing tonight? Did Angie provide you with a description of Lil?" Joe Clay asked.

"Everything I do or see is a writing idea, and no, the women of Paradise didn't look like that. Her ancestors came from that brothel in downtown Spanish Fort. The one without a bit of class," she leaned her head back and unpinned the corsage, which looked more than a little limp.

"Oh? So you get your ideas from everything. Does that include a fellow who got an A tonight on his looks?" Joe Clay asked.

"Sure. You're the hero in my book," she said without thinking.

"Really?" he asked.

"No, not really. Haven't you ever read a book? It says all the characters in this book are entirely fiction and bear no resemblance to anyone living or dead," she covered her own mistake.

"Strange, in that one book you wrote, *The Lady's Slipper*, I could have sworn the villain was a spiced up picture of Pete Lopas," he said, wishing the foot of space between them could be erased and he could drape his arm around her shoulders.

"When did you read my book?" she asked.

"Which one?" he asked right back.

"Any of them?" She was amazed. She knew some men read her novels, but not many stepped up to the plate and admitted it.

"I read the first one right after the Gulf War. I was on my

way home from Iraq and found it in the gift shop right beside my terminal. Kept me entertained for the long hours. I've read them all, at one time or other, some of them more than once," he said.

"Well, thank you. That's quite a compliment," she said.

"Momma, are you going to come up and tuck us all in?" Luna's tired voice called from the hallway.

Mary Jane sighed.

"Your feet have to be tired. Let me do it," Joe Clay said.

"You are a knight in shining armor," she said. He was already out of the room when she remembered that he wasn't the man of the house. He wasn't the girls' father and tucking them in was her job. She started to jump up but didn't. Just this once she'd enjoy what it would be like if Martin hadn't left. If he had stayed in the marriage for the long haul.

Joe Clay kissed both Luna and Endora on the forehead, told them they'd looked like princesses in their pretty frilly dresses, and turned out the light, leaving the door slightly ajar. Neither of them liked a shut door. In the next room he kissed Rae and Bo and tip-toed out of the room, switching off the light as he left. They were both already sound asleep, three kittens on one bed, two on the other. Tertia told him how handsome he'd looked and got two kisses. Ophelia said she'd never had so much fun in her whole life and she wanted a wedding just like that one, but if her mother invited Angie she was going to elope. Ursula had the covers pulled up to her chin, the rascal of a pimple shining on her chin as she snored lightly, more like the loud purrs of the mother cat lying on her feet than a real snore.

Joe Clay found Mary Jane fast asleep on the sofa. Her high-heeled shoes were under the coffee table, her necklace and earrings in the candy dish on top of the coffee table.

She'd removed the clip from her hair and that mass of naturally black hair fanned out over the end of the sofa, some of it falling in a cascade almost to the floor. Joe Clay gently raised her head and placed a throw pillow under it, covered her with a throw, and kissed her on the forehead.

At that moment he would have given his stocks and bonds portfolio to kiss her awake and bare his soul to her. To tell her how proud he'd been to share the pew with her and the girls at the church. How much he still loved her after all those years of trying to get past a silly high school infatuation. But he just gazed his fill of the most beautiful woman in the world and switched off the light as he left the room.

Chapter Eleven

Mary Jane could scarcely believe her eyes. All seven girls were oohing and ahhing as they piled out of the van, in awe of the sight. The whole house looked like the Griswolds' place in that movie, but only for Thanksgiving. Multi–colored silk fall leaves had been: intertwined around the upstairs balcony, the downstairs porch railing, the two front pillars leading up to the porch, even the chains on the swing where an enormous stuffed turkey sat in all his glory. The archway Joe Clay had built to go around the front door for Suzy's wedding was back in place, complete with a big orange bow at the top, silk leaves, and a three foot wooden pilgrim at each side. That didn't even take in the yard decorations. A gazebo off to one side decorated to high heaven. Two park benches arranged to face each other with a small table between them, with a centerpiece of candles and leaves. Wooden turkeys, pumpkins, pilgrims everywhere she looked.

"Ain't it beautiful?" Endora gasped. "Just like Christmas only Thanksgiving."

"Every one of you go to your rooms and wait for me," Mary Jane's voice left no room for discussion. *Drat him!* was all she could think in her moment of rage and confusion. She hated Thanksgiving and here it was, all the memories, the pain, and the humiliation staring her blatantly in the eyes. How dare he presume he could do this to her house without even asking.

She walked into a house with more of the abominable stuff everywhere. She swore if she found one thing near her bedroom, she'd strangle Joe Clay.

"What's wrong? How come the girls went straight to their rooms without saying a word to me? I figured they'd love the decorations. Come and look at the dining room, Mary Jane," he grinned.

"I don't want to look at the dining room, Joe Clay. I want every bit of this out of here. I don't care if you have to work until midnight. If it's not gone by morning, I'll burn it," she said through gritted teeth. "You had no right to do this to my house. And it is my house, not yours."

"Well, pardon me, ma'am, all to the devil. I did it for the girls. Endora wanted to leave up the wedding stuff forever or until Christmas," his heart stopped when it hit the floor and bounced around, a chunk of raw pain.

"Don't do things for the girls. They're my girls. Not yours, Joe Clay. If I want something done for them, I'll ask and then I'll pay you to do it. Just like I'm doing now. You're not their father. You're hired help and that's running on thin ice right now. I cannot believe you did something like this without even asking." Her voice was high and shrill.

"Well, darlin', I'll make it easy on you. I'll slip right through that thin ice. I quit. You paid me last night and since I didn't do anything except try to fix things up for the girls today, you don't owe me a dime. I'll be out of the room in ten minutes. Tell the girls goodbye for me, and I'll be back tomorrow morning while you are all at church to take down the decorations. Thanksgiving was my mother's favorite holiday. It all belonged to her. Don't you dare burn a single leaf." He threw the box of matches on the foyer table beside the candles he'd just lit and stormed into his room, every step of his boot heels sounding like cannon fire on the hardwood floors.

She glared at the gold candle in a gorgeous centerpiece arrangement on her foyer table. A million memories flooded her mind and heart. Not one of them pleasant. The gold candle on the coffee table in the living room of her Dallas home, flickering its last when Martin told her he was leaving her for Caitlin. The empty, gnawing pain when she had to climb the stairs and tell the girls their father wasn't going to be with them for Thanksgiving dinner that day.

"Good-bye, Mary Jane," Joe Clay said as he passed her, careful not to even let his duffel bag touch her.

She just stared at him as if he were a serial killer without saying a word.

"What's happening?" Ursula asked Tertia, who'd slipped back into the bedroom.

"It was a big fight. The biggest one yet. He got his stuff out of his room and he's leaving. We've got to stop him. All of us need to get out on the upstairs porch and wave at him so he won't leave," she started for the french doors.

Ophelia threw herself across the doors, her hands outstretched to keep Tertia from her task. "We can't do that. They need to make up without us. If they can't do that, then it won't work, bad as we all want it to."

"What are you talking about? He's leaving. We can't let him leave. He'll never come back. He didn't know that

Momma don't like Thanksgiving. We never told him that we don't even eat turkey or watch the parade. That we eat sandwiches and ice cream and play Monopoly," Ursula said.

"We can't be here forever," Ophelia said. "If it can't work for all eternity then we don't even want it to work. Momma couldn't take another divorce. It would drive her mad . . . mad, I tell you!" She threw up her hands in the most dramatic effort she'd ever had to portray. "All of us will grow up and get married. Beautiful weddings right here in Paradise. But if they have to have us to settle their fights, what happens then? They'll divorce. Divorce, I tell you. So 'tis a far better thing if it won't work for it to happen now before another holiday is ruined for Momma."

"But I want Joe Clay to come to Thanksgiving. And I want us to watch the parade and eat turkey and . . ." Endora crossed her arms over her chest, stuck out her lower lip, and pouted.

Luna did the same. "Me, too."

"We all did," Rae stroked a kitten's fur. "But Ophelia is right. What if he left her, after we are all gone, on Mother's Day?"

Bo shuddered. "Then we couldn't even buy her roses."

"Vote?" Ursula said, even though it was too late to bring Joe Clay back. The big black truck had already spun out of the driveway, leaving nothing in its wake but a cloud of dust.

"What for? He's gone," Tertia rolled her eyes. All that sneaky spying and still Joe Clay had left. Not one of them had stood with her in trying to stop him.

"To not meddle. To let them work it out or forget our original plan," Ursula said. "All for meddling raise your hand."

Tertia's and Endora's reached for the sky.

"All those who think Ophelia is right and we'd better stay out of it so Joe Clay don't run off with someone else on

Mother's Day after we're all gone, raise your hand," Ursula said.

All seven hands went up.

"Tertia, you and Endora can't vote both ways," Ursula said.

"Yes, I can," Endora's pout turned into a quiver. "I vote that we need to stay out of it in case what you said is true. I don't want to ruin Mother's Day. But I do want to meddle. I don't want to not ever hug Joe Clay again or talk to him."

"And I don't want to stop spying," Tertia hugged her youngest sister close to her side.

"Then the vote is in. We won't meddle this time, but if Joe Clay comes back you can still hug him and Tertia can still spy," Ursula declared.

When their mother knocked on the door, they were all sprawled out on and around the bed listening to a Shania Twain CD, keeping time with their toes and fingertips.

"What's going on?" Mary Jane's voice was strained at best.

"You told us to come up here and go to our rooms. We just decided to go to Ursula's room and listen to her new CD," Ophelia said. "What's going on with you, Momma?"

"Joe Clay is gone. He said to tell you all good-bye. He'll come take down all this mess tomorrow while we are at church. He won't be coming back," she said. "Now if you'll all come and help me unload the groceries and put them away, I'd appreciate it."

Endora wiped a tear but she didn't say a word. For that Mary Jane was thankful. She didn't know if she could endure weeping plus the pain in her heart.

Each girl carried a sack of groceries into the kitchen where they all stopped, stacking up like dominoes with Mary Jane the last in the row. The rough old kitchen table was covered with a ecru-colored tablecloth, ironed to perfection with brightly colored fall leaves intricately embroidered all around the edges. A crocheted shell stitch, in variegated colors ranging from the brilliant burgundy of a black maple tree to the golden yellow of a setting sun, finished the edge. Flickers of lit candles strewn down the middle of the table in every kind of holder imaginable, from the finest crystal to an old wooden one made from a factory thread spool, cast a soft glow over the whole kitchen.

"Ain't it beautiful," Luna whispered in awe.

Endora broke into sobs, set her sack on the floor and ran up the stairs, slamming her bedroom door, the noise breaking the silence. Still no one else moved or said a word, all of them mesmerized by the sight before them.

"I'll go take care of her," Ophelia set her bag down and trudged upstairs, her foot fall heavy in Mary Jane's ears.

To think she'd threatened to burn something as lovely as that tablecloth. His mother had made it, she was sure. Sitting evening after evening, needle in hand as she embroidered those leaves on the finest linen she could find. Then crocheting that edge. Conflicting emotions rattled around in her body like one of the ghosts in the huge old Baker Hotel. Nothing but emptiness and lots of room.

"Would you please blow those candles out, Ursula?" Mary Jane said, her own voice strange in her ears.

"I can't," Ursula sobbed behind her as she, too, turned tail and ran upstairs. She didn't slam her door but Mary Jane wished she would have.

"I'll do it, Momma," Tertia said. "Oh, look, Joe Clay left a candle putter outer." She picked up the snuffer shaped like a turkey and carefully extinguished each of the candles, counting aloud as she did. "One for each of us, Momma. Wasn't that nice of Joe Clay? Eight candles." Tertia's eyes filled with tears. "I think I'll just go on up and listen to music a little while if you don't need me anymore?"

"That's fine," Mary Jane nodded.

Luna, Rae and Bo unloaded the sacks, setting all the food on the countertop beside the sink, then silently filed out of the kitchen, their small heads bowed. Their silence deafening, they left Mary Jane with a week's worth of food to put away and a heart so heavy, it could scarcely beat.

I am right, she defended herself as she worked. Joe Clay had no right to barge into her life. None whatsoever. He was a hired hand. Room and board came with the job but it most assuredly did not give him the title to her kids or her house, much less her heart. She'd trusted once and it backfired, tearing her world apart at the seams. She'd barely been able to keep it together enough to function. Long sleepless nights. Tears when she tried to write a love scene. She'd never put herself in that position again. Not ever.

They'd had a late lunch at Chili's so she'd already told the girls they were on their own for supper. Frozen pizzas. Sandwiches. Soup in the microwave. Whatever. Whenever they wanted. So she climbed the stairs to her own bedroom. The silence of the house was overpowering. The girls must be listening to CDs with earphones. For once she wished she needed to open one of the seven doors, all decorated with something to do with Thanksgiving, and tell someone, anyone, to turn down their music. Just to be able to start a conversation, hopefully that didn't revolve around why Joe Clay wasn't there and why she'd been so mean to him.

She threw herself across the king-sized bed and stared at dust particles in the air, floating there as if they had no place to go in the sunbeams streaming through the glass door. Indian summer. That's what they called this time of year. It came on with vengeance after the first few days of fall. One last ditch effort to show the world that summer wasn't finished in Texas. Steamy hot. High humidity.

After a few minutes her soul grew restless so she kicked off her shoes and changed from jeans and a button-down oxford shirt into her most worn pair of cut-off jeans and a tank top. When she hung her jeans and shirt back in the closet, her eyes fell on the old off-white fisherman's sweater. She'd kept it after the divorce because it was her favorite fall sweater. The one she grabbed on those cool mornings. Big and comfortable for when she wrote. Nothing to confine her. Reminded her of the good years with Martin.

The time before they were married and she hadn't brought a jacket. He'd taken it off right there in the park and put it on her. The kisses were gentle that followed. All the nights she slept in it when he had to work late. She took it off the hanger and hugged it close to her chest.

"Why?" she mumbled.

Then as if the heavens opened up and answered her question, she threw the thing on the floor. Like the sweater, she'd hung on to the false hope that someday Martin would come to his senses. He'd wake up and realize he had seven little girls that needed him. A woman who'd stood beside him through the tough times. Who'd worked and put him through medical school. And right that moment, Mary Jane realized what she'd done.

"No!" she whispered hoarsely.

Yes, her conscience said loudly. She'd closed off her heart to everyone. Kept her life open for her girls. Had she ever asked them if they wanted a traditional Thanksgiving? Not one time. She'd just declared that next year that they were making a new tradition and no one objected. And for four years, they'd ignored the holiday.

She picked up the sweater and carried it downstairs.

Martin still ruled her life and the idea of it nauseated her. She fell onto the couch, still clutching the sweater, leaning her head back and letting the memories come. A jumbled mess of them. Not in any order. A vision of Martin wearing the sweater. One of his face when Ursula was born. The indifference when Luna and Endora came into the world. That fatal Thanksgiving when he marched into the house after staying, supposedly, at the hospital with a critical patient all night, to tell her he'd filed for divorce. The smell of the turkey roasting in the oven. Pecan pies cooling on the counter. Hot rolls ready to go in the oven at the last minute. All the girls dressed up in fall-colored velvet dresses.

The sweater had been in her closet when he cleaned his out. And she'd held onto it even when she sent the things he'd forgotten to his new address. The one he shared with Caitlin. She tossed it on the end of the sofa, staring at it as if it were a rattlesnake. It was time to let go. Martin wasn't coming back to her. To think that he might. To hang on like she'd been doing, was nothing short of subconscious craziness. She'd been goofy as an outhouse rat for four long years.

It was time to put the past behind her, to get on with life. To enjoy a Thanksgiving holiday with her girls. To end this silence.

"Hey girls," she yelled from the bottom of the stairs. "Want to build a fire out back and have a weenie roast?"

Ursula opened her door and cautiously peeked down at her mother. "That would be nice, Momma, but not if you're going to burn up all the decorations."

"No, silly girl. Joe Clay is coming tomorrow morning and take them all down. I'm not going to burn them. We'll just build a fire with sticks. You can all help gather them," she smiled brightly.

"I do," Ophelia said from behind Ursula. "Can we do smores?"

"I think we've got all the stuff. You go in the kitchen and gather up the goods. The rest of the girls and I'll gather sticks and start the fire blazing," Mary Jane said.

One by one they came out of their rooms. One by one they began talking again. Pretty soon giggles and noise filled Paradise.

They gathered sticks and dry leaves and built a fire just before dusk. They cooked wieners until they were charred and ate them on cold buns with mustard and relish. They roasted marshmallows until the outside was black and the inside a gooey mess and got them all over their fingertips.

"This is fun, Momma. It's really too hot for a fire but it's been fun," Tertia told her. "But now I'm ready to go get a bath. I feel all grimy and dirty and sticky."

"Me, too," Ophelia said.

"Then the bunch of you go on inside and get your baths. Three at a time. Two in the tubs, one in the downstairs shower. When you're all done, call me from the upstairs balcony and I'll shovel dirt on the fire to put it out. I'd like to sit here for a while and watch the flames," she said.

"But Momma, you're already sweating," Tertia said.

"I know, sweetheart," she kissed her daughter on the girl's sweaty forehead, tasting salt and smelling wood smoke and relish.

When they'd all ran like gazelles into the house, she withdrew the sweater from the paper sack she'd hidden it inside and tossed it on the fire. "Good-bye Martin. I wish you well. I forgive you but I do not want you back," she said and watched the fire consume every last thread of the sweater, leaving nothing but a very very small pile of ashes.

They watched *Shrek* for the hundredth time before they went to bed. Wearing summer pajamas. Sprawled out all over the living room floor with pillows and favorite stuffed animals. Mary Jane's mind wandered during the movie. She'd cook Thanksgiving dinner this year and they'd watch the parade on television. They might even get dressed up and put candles on the table. But that was enough for one year. None of this family–decorated–to–the–hilt stuff. One step at a time. That's all a baby took when it began to walk. Just one step at a time and she was starting all over in this business of forgiveness and hearts.

She tucked them all in bed a few minutes past ten and went to her room. She picked up her chapter book and thought about the last three chapters she needed to finish for *The Reckless Knight*. At least she tried to think about it. Mostly what she did was doodle on the blank page before her. She'd been wrong but how did one undo a wrong? Especially when Joe Clay was already gone to who knew where. She'd fired him. Thrown his efforts back at him with hurricane force, threatened to burn his mother's tablecloth. She laid the chapter book aside and picked up her Bible to read tomorrow's Sunday school lesson. A lesson from Psalms 30:8–10 where David asked God, "Why me?"

She read the lesson and laid it aside. *Why me? Indeed!* But the answer came in the fact that sometimes a person had to fall flat to be able to see what they couldn't see standing erect. It took a fight with Joe Clay to bring her to her senses. And he was coming back to Paradise tomorrow morning to take down all the decorations he'd put up. God would forgive her for not going to church, she was sure. Because she was going to beg for Joe Clay's forgiveness.

She fell asleep with a smile on her face.

* * *

Joe Clay spent the night playing poker with his card buddies. When he mentioned getting a motel room, they'd teased him about giving up the life out in Paradise. That led to jokes about how a man could only stand so much Paradise anyway. And how did he ever put up with that many kids? It was near daylight by the time the game ended so he pulled his truck into the grocery store parking space and waited until it was time to go to Mary Jane's and reclaim all his mother's decorations. There didn't seem to be a lot of need to pay for a motel for only five hours use. He certainly couldn't sleep.

He waited until he was sure they'd all be at church and drove the seventeen miles to Spanish Fort, down the long lane lined with bare pecan trees, to the house. He was stepping up on the porch when Mary Jane cleared her throat. Just the sight of her sitting there on the porch swing beside that big stuffed fabric turkey made his mouth go dry.

"Could we talk?" she asked.

"Guess we done already talked too much," he said. He'd take the archway, flowers, bow, and all to the truck. He could take the leaf swags off later.

"Guess I did," she said. "Please, Joe Clay, I'm asking you to please come and sit beside me and this turkey. I need to get something off my chest."

"Guess you did a fine job of that yesterday," he told her. His feet were glued to the porch as solidly as if he'd fastened them there with ten penny nails.

"Yes, I did. And now . . . blast it all to the devil. Joe Clay, come over here and sit down. I want to apologize. I want to beg you to stay. I want to have Thanksgiving and I want you to leave all this alone. I was wrong," she all but shouted.

"Well, well. You think a little outburst like that is going to heal up all those mean things you said?" he asked.

"Probably not. But you said you'd stay until Christmas. There's still work to be done and we shook on it," she said.

He slumped in the small space beside her, careful not to touch her shoulder or her leg. They sat in uncomfortable silence, pushing the swing together. Not fast. Not slow. Steady, as if they'd spent years sitting there on Sunday morning.

Joe Clay cleared his throat and said, "I've been thinking."

"Oh no," Mary Jane shook her head. "That's a dangerous place to go, now isn't it?"

"Now what makes you say that?" He brushed his gray hair back with his finger tips. It was getting too long. He'd have to drop by the barber shop soon.

"Last time you said something like that, I remember a bunch of us ending up in Mineral Wells touring a haunted hotel at dusk," she said.

"Alzheimers hasn't reared its ugly head prematurely in Mary Jane Marsh Simmons. She remembers everything," a grin tickled the corners of his mouth in spite of the fact that he wanted to stay mad at her.

"My family lives to be a hundred and dies of natural causes and they have the memory of an elephant. No Alzheimers here," she told him.

"Well, I been thinking . . . anyway! I played poker all night and slept in my truck until time to come out here, Mary Jane. Had about five hours of time to do nothing but think since I was too angry and too wired up to sleep. I should have asked you first. I didn't know you hated Thanksgiving and it's none of my business why you hate a holiday but I got a notion it's got to do with that ex–husband of yours. Endora liked the house all decorated up for the wedding last week. Thanksgiving was my mother's favorite holiday in the whole world. That's when her kids all came home. Didn't matter what part of the world I was in, if it was humanly possible,

I flew home for Thanksgiving. My two older brothers and their kids all came in and Momma cooked for weeks before the holiday. Because Dad knew how much she loved it, he made her something new every year. There were all these boxes and boxes of Thanksgiving decorations in the storage shed in Nocona. And I just thought I'd surprise the whole bunch of you."

"Well, that you sure did," she said, suddenly liking the feel of Joe Clay sitting beside her and the big turkey.

"Mary Jane, why didn't you remarry?" He asked bluntly.

"Wow. One minute we're discussing turkeys and the next we're discussing . . ." she giggled nervously.

"Turkeys!" He finished the line for her.

"Guess you're right. I haven't remarried because there's seven little girls in the house. Most men run when they come face to face with that. You did and you were just hired help. Then there's the fact that I write romance books. That scares them off for some reason. Then there's the last fact. I haven't wanted to remarry, Joe Clay. I got burned bad the first time around. After I fall off the bike, it takes a while to get back on," she said.

"I see," he said. But he didn't. Kids weren't an issue. Good girls they were. Smart. Full of spit and vinegar but no one was going to lead a one of them where they didn't want to go. Mary Jane had done a fantastic job of raising them alone. Her job was writing. So what? She did it well and he was proud of her for all her accomplishments. What would it take for someone to come along and change her mind? Make her want to remarry? He'd have to think on that one awhile.

"Will you stay and finish the job? I apologize and I've worked through the problem. All night I've worked through it. Came face to face with it and took care of it," she told him.

"I'll stay," he said. If she'd asked him to stand on his head cross–eyed in hot ashes he would have done it. Not that he wanted her to know that but he was down right in love with the woman, and he'd fully well planned on still being there when the family got out of church that morning. Only he'd figured he and Mary Jane would have another rousting good argument when he informed her that she wasn't breaking their verbal contract. She'd promised him work until Christmas and he'd have it or she'd face a lawsuit.

Six weeks. That's what he had to change her mind about him.

"Thank you, Joe Clay. Hey girls, he says he'll stay," she called out in a normal voice.

Girls whooped and hollered and came running from the side yard. Endora bailed halfway across the porch into his lap. Luna patted one arm. Rae and Bo fought for space behind him. The three older girls just stood back, their eyes twinkling.

Joe Clay thought he'd truly died and found Paradise.

Chapter Twelve

"But Momma," Endora begged.

"No ifs, ands, or buts," Mary Jane told her. "Joe Clay is a grown man and he's got plans to go to Austin to spend the holiday with his brother. You're not going to put him in a difficult place by asking him to stay here with us. We'll have Thanksgiving. A turkey with all the trimmings, and even watch the Thanksgiving Day parade. But you're not going to ruin Joe Clay's day with his family."

"Then I'll ask Ophelia to pray," Endora said with a toss of her blonde curls. "When Baptist nuns pray God listens, cause there ain't too many of them."

"Ophelia can pray until she gets calluses on her knees but Joe Clay is still going to his brother's house, so don't you try threatening me with that," Mary Jane turned Endora around and walked her to the foot of the stairs. "Now you go to your room and finish writing your spelling words ten times each."

Mary Jane kept the giggle inside as she prepared *The Reckless Knight* manuscript for mailing the next day. Endora

159

could easily be a witch, but even a witch couldn't get what she wanted with her sister's prayers.

Mary Jane had promised herself that if she finished it by Thanksgiving she'd take a month long vacation. Spend time decorating the house for Christmas, buying gifts, maybe even reading three or four big thick books herself. At least she didn't have to decorate for Thanksgiving. Joe Clay had done a fine job of that. She might need to hit the stores right after the holiday and buy half price decorations for the next year, though. She had an idea that Endora was going to want it to look the same next year.

"Hey, got a minute?" Joe Clay said.

She jumped with fright and shivered with something she thought she had under complete control—desire.

"Didn't mean to startle you," Joe Clay scanned the area. No girls. He could hear music upstairs, the television going in the living room, but no girls in the formal dining room. He stepped in close enough to inhale the coconut smell of her hair. By shutting his eyes he could feel the warmth of the sun in the islands, the smell of coconut, the lazy way of life wrapping him up in its arms like a lover.

"Sure, I've got a minute. Manuscript is ready to go tomorrow morning," she tapped the two inch stack of copy paper with rubber bands securing the pages together. She whipped around to find Joe Clay so close that his face blurred.

All he had to do was lean in slightly and their lips met. The sizzle fried his senses. His imagination set them right down in the middle of white sand with a gentle wind spreading the aroma of coconut all around them. Mixed emotions shot through Mary Jane. She didn't want this. She wanted it to never end. The girls might walk in and see Joe Clay kissing her. She didn't care who saw the kiss. She forgot it all and kissed him back, wrapping her arms around his neck and softly massaging his neck as she enjoyed the embrace.

"I think maybe that took more than a minute," she tried humor to cover the blush flowing across her cheeks.

"What?" he murmured, tangling his hands in her long, black hair, nuzzling the inside of her neck, enjoying the quiver down her spine as he did.

"You asked me if I had a minute, Joe Clay," she stepped out of the circle of his arms.

"Oh, that," he said. "But hey, you got a minute?" He looked at her and grinned.

"Never knew that to be a pickup line," she smiled back.

"Neither did I or I'd have used it before now," he told her. "I'm getting ready to close up that doorway from my bedroom over into your office. I just want you to come in and really make up your mind about it. I'm thinking you might want to leave it, Mary Jane. Someday when the kids are all grown and gone, you might get tired of climbing those stairs. It would be easy to close the bedroom doors upstairs and not have to go up there every day. You could have your bedroom where mine is and your office right off it."

She'd never thought of that. Someday when the kids were grown and gone. Good grief! That would happen. They'd all be gone before she could blink twice. Ursula would be out of high school in five years. Then the domino effect would begin. Ophelia, six years. Tertia, eight. Rae and Bo, nine. Luna and Endora, ten. In only one decade she'd be left alone to rattle around in this big old house except when they all came home for holidays from college.

"Did a goose just step on your grave?" Joe Clay asked.

"I think it did." Mary Jane remembered the old adage. When a person shivered from head to toe with no reason, it was said that they felt a goose step on their grave from another life.

"What on earth were you thinking about?" Joe Clay ushered her down the hall toward his bedroom by placing his hand on the small of her back.

"My girls growing up," she told him, honestly. "Somehow I'd just figured they'd always be here. Be here at the age they are now. They are going to grow up just like we did, Joe Clay. Oh. My. Lord. What if they get some wild hair when they're seniors and decide to go tour a haunted hotel? They could fall off that balcony."

Joe Clay laughed deep in his chest, knowing what she was talking about. She'd gone out on the top floor balcony and walked right on top of the railing. Fourteen floors up and all the other girls about to need smelling salts. He could still see her. The hot Texas breeze whipping that hip length black hair around her face. Her arms out for balance. He'd loved her that night; he loved her still. He'd been too afraid of rejection to tell her then but his courage was building.

"You know what I'm talking about?" She stood in the middle of his spotless room. A dust mite would be afraid to cross the threshold into his room, she was sure.

"I remember. You were going to walk from one end to the other but the tour guide almost stroked out when he finally got out there with us so you nimbly jumped back on the balcony and we all had to listen to a breathless lecture from our sixty year old tour guide," Joe Clay said.

"The sins of mothers," she mumbled.

"Don't let the future mar the present. Nor the past," he told her.

"You're right, Joe Clay. Leave the doorway. When are you going to start pulling the plaster and lathing off?" She wanted to think of something other than the impetuosity of invincible high school seniors.

"Monday. I figure I can get it all torn off and ready for sheet rock before I go to Austin. I leave on Wednesday afternoon. Back on Sunday. The next Monday I've got a couple of men hired to help me hang the sheet rock. Got to have help if I'm going to get that bonus," he said.

That big king-sized bed was too close for her to walk into his arms. The door was too far away to casually kick shut with her foot so the girls wouldn't think they could come running into the room. She ignored both and slid across the room and into his chest. "Hold me, Joe Clay. Just hold me like a friend and erase all the fears."

"I can hold you, honey. I can hold you forever, but you've got to erase the fears. I'll walk with you through them as far as you'll let me," he whispered.

"Fair enough," she whispered back.

"Momma? Momma? Where are you?" Ophelia yelled all the way down the hall.

"And I was worried they'd never grow up," Mary Jane sighed as she went through the door into her office. By the time Ophelia threw open the door to the office without knocking, Mary Jane was staring at her computer screen.

On Monday it began to rain and the temperature dropped to thirty-four degrees. Mary Jane spent the whole day curled up on the sofa with a big, thick romance book by her favorite author. Cinnamon-scented candles burned on the coffee table. Joe Clay had started a fire for her in the fireplace. She'd thrown open the drapes to enjoy the gray, rainy day, and had a bowl of pretzels close at hand, along with a quart jar of iced tea.

Joe Clay whistled while he worked, noisily. He listened to a Billy Ray Cyrus CD. Cyrus sang about leaving the house with her . . . he was talking about divorce, but it caused Joe Clay to think of the kiss last week, when Mary Jane had been worried about the girls growing up and pulling some of the same stunts she had. Joe Clay would be leaving, even though it wasn't divorce. The kisses were nice, more than nice. They were everything he'd ever imagined. Cyrus was begging in the song for one last thrill with the lady of his life, saying that he would always love her, asking that she go with him for one last drive to take one last look at the shining stars, and for one last kiss, one last thrill. Joe Clay sang along, his heart truly in the song. Only he didn't want one last thrill. He wanted one beginning thrill that would lead on to more and more, until they both slid into eternity together yelling, "Whooppeee!"

Mary Jane heard the whistling and then the singing as Joe Clay sang along with Billy Ray, one of her favorite country singers. When Cyrus started singing "Bluegrass State of Mind," she shut her eyes. Listening to the words, she kept time with her fingers on the book. Cyrus said he was in a bluegrass state of mind, that he missed that Kentucky girl that he left behind. Did Joe Clay ever really miss her when he was off fighting wars and doing all those covert things?

"Now where did that come from?" She picked up the book and focused on the words but they were blurry.

By mid-afternoon the temperature had dropped to thirty degrees and the rain all but stopped, barely a nice, slow drizzle. Joe must have had the CD on constant repeat because it kept playing over and over. Not that Mary Jane minded one bit. She finally laid the book aside and let her mind wander through the songs, using them to analyze her own feelings; past, present, future.

The school bus arrived at least an hour early and seven

girls, all bundled up in coats, scarves, and gloves rushed through the front door with the news that there would be no school the next day.

"Why?" Mary Jane helped them hang up coats, line boots up on a mat beside the front door, and hang scarves and gloves on the pegs above the boots.

"Momma, haven't you looked outside? It's freezing out there. The bus slipped and skidded all the way down our lane. The driver said he was glad we was the last ones he had to bring home," Ursula said.

"Oh, my," Mary Jane said.

"Didn't you have the television or the radio on today?" Rae asked.

"No, Joe Clay was listening to Billy Ray and I was reading all day. Why?" Mary Jane answered.

"Just that there's an ice storm on the way. The principal said the rain is going to freeze and the trees are going to freeze and we'll be lucky if the electricity don't go out," Ursula told her mother.

Mary Jane picked up the remote from the coffee table and switched the television to the Weather Channel. The announcer told them to lay in supplies until at least Friday. The temperature would continue to drop through Thanksgiving Day but Friday the sun was expected to shine and begin to melt the oncoming ice.

"Have we got everything for our Thanksgiving?" Ophelia asked.

"Yes, but . . ." Mary Jane thought about Joe Clay and his flight.

At supper Endora asked Joe Clay if he was still going to Austin.

"Of course. I've driven to the airport in worse conditions than this, honey. That old black truck out there can drive through anything," he assured her, wishing with everything he possessed that someone around the table would just ask him to stay in Paradise for the holiday. He'd forfeit his ticket, make a phone call, and be happy as a sow in a fresh summer mud wallow if Mary Jane would look up and invite him to Thanksgiving dinner.

"Ophelia, you've got to pray harder," Endora whispered to her sister that evening.

"It will take a miracle, little sister, but Baptist nuns believe in miracles, don't they? So I shall pray tonight for a miracle," Ophelia patted her head. "Now go on back to bed. Joe Clay will be here on Thanksgiving. He will eat turkey with us and Momma will see a new tradition."

"Ophelia, did you pray that the ice would come and we would have an extra day out of school?" Endora narrowed her big blue eyes at her older sister.

"No, I did not," Ophelia said. "But I would have if I'd have thought of it."

Joe Clay pushed the button on his CD. Billy Ray's voice came through the speakers telling him that the secrets of the treasures of heaven could be found in the heart of a woman. He picked up a mug and started to sip the lukewarm remains of black coffee, only to find it empty. He couldn't remember when he'd drank the last of it, so lost in thought was he as he watched the slow, slow drizzle build a layer of ice on everything it touched.

Mary Jane blew the candles out in the living room, picked up the quart jar with only an inch of melted ice and a sliver of lemon left. She made her way to the kitchen, noticing the floor had gotten much, much colder in the last hour. Ice. The crippling weather of the South.

"Looks like we had the same idea," Joe Clay startled her from the darkened kitchen. "Brought my coffee mug to wash it," he explained.

"My tea jar," she raised the quart jar.

"Still drinking out of a mason jar? Why M. J. Marsh, I figured you'd be using crystal flutes from Waterford," he teased, leaning against the cabinet.

Lord, why did he have to come in here without a shirt on? She wondered as her eyes adjusted to the darkness. "Some habits die hard. I've got this notion that the mason jar keeps my tea cold longer. One thing for sure, it holds more." She could see the muscles rippling down his abs, the tattoo on his bicep, his silver hair shining in the semi–darkness.

"Guess we're in for a stinker of an ice storm. Haven't lived through one of these since we were kids. Sophomores weren't we? And it was in late January. Not an early one like now," Joe Clay looked out the window to keep from drawing her into his arms and kissing her until he got tired of feeling her there, or died, whichever came first. He figured it would be death.

"What is this?" She reached up and traced the outline of the tattoo.

"Special forces tattoo," he said hoarsely, the whole knife suddenly on fire.

"What does that mean?" She asked.

"I could tell you but then I'd have to kill you," he repeated the age old line in a ragged whisper. "How 'bout I don't tell you and just kiss you instead?"

He didn't give her time to answer but drew her to his bare chest, tilted her chin back, and heated up the whole room with a series of kisses.

Mary Jane dreamed of Joe Clay that night for the first time. She dreamed that she was teetering on the balcony railing fourteen stories up at the Baker Hotel and lost her balance. She began to fall and it was Joe Clay's strong arms that pulled her to safety. She awoke breathless, shivering, to the sound of rifle fire not far from her house. She sat straight up in bed and threw off the covers. Looked at the alarm clock to find it blank. Turned on the lamp beside her bed. The bulb was shot.

"No, it's not, the electricity is gone," she moaned, jerking the covers back around her neck. She had no choice but to get up and figure out what she was going to do now. She had decided on electric heating and cooling so that left the fireplace in the living room and the gas cook stove in the kitchen. The water heater upstairs had been replaced by an electric one. Thank goodness the downstairs bathroom had a heater of its own and that one was still run by gas. After this morning, as she hopped around on the cold floor, trying to get dressed, she might always keep a gas one downstairs. Where was all that heat and fire she'd felt in the kitchen last night as she and Joe Clay stole those steamy kisses? She felt her lips. No, they were as cold as the rest of her body.

"Good mornin'," Joe Clay said when she reached the kitchen. He'd shut the door and had it toasty warm, all four burners lit and the oven door open. "I started a blaze in the fireplace. Glad for that cord of wood on the back porch you had brought in last week. It'll last you through the week, I'm thinking."

"Thanks, Joe Clay," she said. "I'll get breakfast started."

"Momma, I'm freezing," Endora opened the door and slipped inside. "Hold me, Joe Clay. Why is everything cold except the kitchen?"

Joe Clay reached to pick her up and a clap that sounded like half the roof had collapsed sent her jumping into his arms. He and Mary Jane both ran to the front door to see what had made so much noise.

"Uh–oh," Endora said.

An enormous limb from the first pecan tree toward the house in the lane had broken and lay across the lane. Another snap brought still yet another one on the other side of the lane to the ground, both of the limbs a tangle of branches and ice barricading the lane.

"I have to go talk to Ophelia," Endora wiggled out of Joe Clay's arms. "I'm a believer, now."

"What's she talking about?" Joe Clay asked.

"Who knows? Girls keep secrets from mothers," she looked at the disaster in front of her. "How are you going to get out of here tomorrow morning?"

"Good question," he said. Prayers did get answered in a strange way, now didn't they?

"Oh, Joe Clay, I'm so sorry you can't go be with your family," she put a hand over her mouth when she realized what she was truly looking at.

"I'm not," Endora said from the top of the stairs. "Joe Clay, will you please have Thanksgiving dinner with us? If the 'tricity stays off all week, we won't get to watch the parade, but we're going to have turkey and pecan pie."

"I'd be honored, if it's all right with your mother," Joe Clay looked deeply into Mary Jane's dark green eyes.

"And what would I do? Tell you that you have to walk a hundred miles to Dallas? Of course you'll stay and eat with us," Mary Jane huffed.

"Yipppeee," Endora danced down the hallway to awaken Ophelia and tell her about their miracle.

"I'm sorry," Joe Clay said honestly to Mary Jane.

"What for?" she asked.

"I know you and the girls like to have this holiday alone. I'll be intruding but there's nothing I can do about it," he said.

"Oh, hush, Joe Clay. We're starting a new tradition this year anyway. You are more than welcome to share it. Unless the electricity comes back on in two days, though, we're not going to watch the parade. Good grief, what are we going to do?"

"I suggest the girls bring down bedding from their rooms. The living room is huge. They can each claim a section of land. Their comforters will be their own private rooms, then they can roll up in them at night. I'll keep the fire stoked up good and strong so they'll be semi-warm. We can play games with them in the kitchen. My power tools won't work anyway so I'll lose a couple of days' work, but I'll help keep them entertained. Now how about we start up some breakfast? Sausage, gravy, and biscuits. Something good and heavy to stick to their bones and keep them warm," he said.

"You got all the answers?" She gladly made her way to the kitchen.

"Not to the important ones," he mumbled as he followed her.

"Oh, no! Oh, no!" Ursula exclaimed after Rae said grace.

"What? Momma didn't burn the gravy did she?" Luna sniffed her plate.

"No, I just realized there is no electricity. No television. No music. No movies. No Playstation Two. What are we going to do?" Ursula asked.

"That's nothing. No hair dryer. No lights to see how to put that stuff on your pimple if you get one. No sunshine to even help us see ourselves in the bathroom mirror," Tertia groaned.

"Worse than that. No hot water!" Ophelia gasped.

"Only downstairs. The hot water down here is still heated

by gas," Mary Jane smiled. "We are lucky. We have a fire-place that will give us a little warmth. Plenty of wood to keep it fed. We have a gas cook stove so we can have Thanksgiving dinner and a warm kitchen to have it in. We've got hot water still downstairs so we can all have showers at night and wash dishes."

"But we were going to eat in the big dining room, all fancy," Luna said.

"Well, we'll be thankful to have a warm kitchen," Mary Jane told them.

"Why did this have to happen to me?" Ursula moaned.

"Little girl, please say that quietly. If this whole part of the state finds out this calamity happened just to punish you, then I'm afraid they'll be standing out in front of the house by noon demanding I send you out so they can stone you to death. That way it won't ever happen again," Mary Jane whispered in the most evil voice she could conjure up.

"Momma!" Ursula shuddered. "You know what I mean!"

"Of course I do. Now think about what you can do to entertain yourselves all day. There's room for a Monopoly game here in the kitchen. Joe Clay suggested you each bring your comforters and set up a camp for each of you in the living room. We'll light candles and fill every hurricane lamp we can find with that scented lamp oil in the hall closet, and you can read. That's what I intend to do," Mary Jane said. "Right after we eat and the whole bunch of you help with these dishes. Then tonight I'm going to start baking. A banana nut cake has to sit at least two days prior to cutting for the flavors to blend. I can make my cranberry salad and maybe even a couple of batches of pecan sandies."

"Can I help?" Ursula asked petulantly. "I'd rather cook as read or play boring Monopoly."

"Sure, you can," Mary Jane said. "But remember, Joe Clay

and I are not the entertainment committee. You can treat this as an exciting adventure or a long, boring experience. It's up to you."

She wondered who she was talking to even as the words came out of her mouth. Since August, she had treated her life as an exciting adventure. Writing a novel that literally sped out of her fingers. Remodeling the old brothel into a wonderful home. Arguing with Joe Clay. Kissing him. Touching that tattoo. Excitement. Had there been a boring day?

Not yet.

"You know one time I got in a situation like this. Only difference was where this is colder than . . ." he almost gave them a military expression that would have been totally unfit for little girls' ears ". . . a well digger's belt buckle in the heart of Alaska," he finally said. "It was hotter than blue blazes where I was. But we didn't have any electricity. Just a tent to keep a bit of shade over our heads through the day. We were told to wait for a week right there. Some of my young men moaned and groaned, wanting to disobey orders and go on ahead with the fight. Take it to the enemy they said. But the others? Now they pulled out cards and played. They reread letters and wrote letters. When the end of the week came the ones who'd fussed around thought it had lasted a year. The ones who'd made wise use of their time couldn't believe it was over."

"Did you save the world that time?" Endora asked.

Joe Clay looked down into adoring blue eyes and swallowed down the lump in his throat. If only those blue eyes were a genetic inheritance from him. "Of course I did, Endora. I saved the world."

"I knew it," she said and asked for more biscuits and gravy. "Luna, you want to play paper dolls with me on our comforter?"

"Sure. We can get out the *Gone With The Wind* ones and 'tend we're back in Tara. Oh, sugar, I just can't decide who I'm goin' to marry," Luna faked a deep southern accent.

Mary Jane giggled.

Joe Clay roared.

The rest of the girls looked at both of them like they were crazy.

On Thanksgiving day they sat in the warm kitchen, a spread laid out before them. Turkey with southern cornbread sage dressing, candied sweet potatoes, baked beans, mashed potatoes and giblet gravy, green beans with potatoes and bacon boiled in them, cranberry salad, fruit salad, and hot rolls. Mary Jane had unpacked her good china and crystal. Candles set at strategic places all around the room cast a soft glow over the whole meal.

They'd dressed for the meal. The girls in their Sunday finery, all except for shoes. Instead they wore warm socks and fluffy house shoes. Joe Clay wore a crisp white shirt and bolo tie with a diamond horseshoe slide. His gray hair was still too long to suit him, but sitting at the other end of the table, Mary Jane thought it was perfect. She'd chosen a long loden green velvet dress with side slits that showed a healthy bit of her long legs. Like the girls she wore thick socks and house shoes instead of the strappy little sandals that matched the dress.

"Before we begin, we'll bow our heads and . . ." Mary Jane tried to remember whose turn it was to do grace.

"And start a new tradition," Joe Clay looked down the table at the most beautiful woman he'd ever known. She'd argue that this was her Thanksgiving table, her kids, her house, he was sure.

"And what's that?" She cocked her head to one side.

"We all hold hands and with one word only, go around the

table. Each of us have to come up with one word describing what we are thankful for. I'll start," he placed his hands on the table. Endora's immediately went into his. Luna's followed on the other side. "Now, we begin. My word is Paradise," he said without taking his eyes off Mary Jane.

Luna said, "Thanksgiving."

"Kittens," Bo said.

A silence as Rae tried to think of one word to express it all. Finally she said, "Love."

Tertia grinned. "Ice."

Mary Jane looked around the table. "Family."

Ursula held her head high and said, "Sisters."

Ophelia winked at Tertia. "Prayers."

Endora didn't even hesitate, "Joe Clay. Oops, that's two words. Then just Joe."

Late that night when the girls had bedded down and the soft sounds of their breathing could be heard around the living room, he and Mary Jane sat on the sofa, both wrapped in a separate quilt.

"That about undid me when Endora said my name in the Thanksgiving round," he said.

"She loves you Joe Clay. Unconditionally. You've given her something she can't remember ever having. A male in the family," Mary Jane said.

"What are we going to do about us?" Joe Clay reached out and took Mary Jane's hand in his. "I'm not going to want to leave. You know that. I've made no bones about how I feel about you."

"Kids? Seven of them," she reminded him.

"I wouldn't care if there was a dozen," he leaned his head back, speaking the truth even if it did terrify him.

"Joe Clay, it's four weeks until Christmas. Let's see what happens in those four weeks," she said.

"You'll open your heart and give it a real try?" he asked, tracing her jaw line with his forefinger.

"I'll do my best. Trusting isn't easy for me," she said.

"Give it a try. Give me a try," he whispered softly in her ear and kissed her, hoping the last thrill he ever knew with her would be the day he slipped away into eternity . . . with the warmth of a kiss still on his lips.

Chapter Thirteen

The big brass door knocker falling heavily brought all seven girls to the foyer to stand in a line. Ursula opened the door like she did every year.

"Girls!" Martin threw open the screen door and began the hugs. One at a time. To each the same words as the previous years. How much they'd grown.

"Mary Jane?" He said when he reached the end of the line and looked up at her sitting halfway up the staircase. "Could I have a word in private?"

"Of course, in my office?" She led the way down the hall to her own private space. "What's on your mind?" She asked after she'd shut the door.

"What can you be thinking about? Bringing my daughters to this podunk mud puddle? To an old brothel, at that? Are you crazy?" He crossed his arms over his chest in defiance.

"Not at all. They've adapted well to the small school system. Not one of them are on drugs or in a gang, as far as I know. Now Ophelia may make you think she is when she begins her 'praise the lord' business, but it's just her grandmother's drama surfacing. The Paradise was big enough to house us all comfortably and the reconstruction is coming along beautifully. Plus there's a wonderful bonus. I found a bunch of old journals up in the attic. I just wrote and sold the most amazing book. It'll be out September, and the movie of it will premiere the following January if all the deadlines are met. So this move has been wonderful for all of us," she said, not one single string pulling in her heart toward him. She crossed the room and knocked on the door into Joe Clay's bedroom, which was finally completed just last week. Until then he'd used the guest room upstairs. Talk about a lot of long nights. Knowing he was right across the hallway. Feeling the warmth of his kisses still on her lips every night. Giving it a chance and liking where it was going.

"Has he gone?" Joe Clay opened the door.

"No, but he's leaving. Martin, I'd like you to meet Joseph Clay Carter. I thought you might like to put a face to the name you're going to hear a lot of in the next twenty-four hours. Joe Clay, this is the girls' father, Martin Simmons. Martin, this is Joe Clay."

Joe Clay held out his hand, shaking with the most flabbergasted man in all of Montague County, he was sure. "I'm glad to meet you, Martin. You've got seven of the most fantastic daughters in the world. You are a lucky man to have them."

"Thank you," Martin finally got out. "A few more words with you?" He said through clenched teeth, looking straight at Mary Jane.

"I'll go tell the girls good-bye. They've already given me

orders about the kittens and Momma cat, but I'm sure they'll need to reinforce them. Besides Endora said she wants one more hug before she leaves," Joe Clay said, towering above Martin and grinning the whole way out of the room.

"Who is he? Endora mentioned a handyman the last time I called. Is he the man?" Martin asked.

"Of course, but he's a lot more than a handyman, let me tell you. I'm in love with the man," Mary Jane said.

"You can't marry a yokel like that, Mary Jane. For heaven's sake, he's just a repairman," Martin all but gasped.

"I didn't say I was going to marry him. He hasn't asked me. But what I can do and what I can't is none of your business. He's been here for all of us. He helped us endure an ice storm with no electricity for five days. He's worked like a fiend getting this house ready so I could have Christmas in Paradise. He's loved me since high school and I was a fool then not to realize what he offered. He's honest and kind, Martin, and I'll do whatever I want," she said. "You don't want those little girls out there except for a twenty-four hour stretch at Christmas. Looks to me like you'd be happy to have someone pick up the slack you leave behind."

"Still bitter at me are you?" He grinned.

"Not at all. I've forgiven you. I hope you and Caitlin have a long and happy life together. Buy a third world country with her money and be king of it. I don't really care what you do. I'm grateful for the years I had with you because it netted me seven little girls. But honey, what I've got right now with Joe Clay is a touch of paradise compared with all of hell when I compare it with what we had. Go enjoy your girls. Give them something big and flashy for their presents to soothe your conscience. Joe Clay will love them for you," she said.

"You still love me," he whispered, reaching out to touch her shoulder.

"No, Martin, I don't," she lifted his hand and dropped it like so much garbage. "Hey girls," she opened the door wide, "throw the switch so you can let your father see the lights."

"How gaudy," he mumbled as the blinking lights filtered through all the windows.

"Look Daddy, it's just like the Griswolds' house in the movies. Joe Clay helped us put it all up. We've got enough lights to make the electric meter run in fast circles. But ain't it pretty?" Endora said from six feet up in the air, inside the circle of Joe Clay's arms.

"I'll have them back by bedtime tomorrow. Caitlin and I are flying out on Christmas Eve. We're spending the holiday with her folks in the south of France."

"Have a wonderful time," Joe Clay shifted Endora into Martin's arms.

He promptly set her on the floor. "Come along girls. We've got a whole night and day planned special for you. Caitlin will be with us tonight, but tomorrow she's got some shopping to do. We'll eat out and see a movie and do some shopping of our own. You girls need to buy her a present."

"Okay," Endora danced out toward the limousine. "Joe Clay took us to buy Momma a present last week. I'll tell you when we get in the car what I bought her. Oh, Daddy, tell the driver to go slow so we can look back and see the lights the whole way down the lane. I just love looking like the Griswolds."

Mary Jane waved from the porch until she couldn't see the limo anymore, her heart lighter than it had been since the night she walked the balcony banister in Mineral Wells,

Texas. Joe Clay slipped up behind her, wrapped her in a soft, warm blanket, scooped her up into his arms and carried her to the porch swing.

She laced her arms around his neck and cuddled down into his lap. An overstuffed, life-sized Santa Claus, sharing the swing with them. "That was good. I feel like I've finally got closure."

"Good," he kissed her forehead. "I've been thinking."

"Oh, no. Are we going to the Baker Hotel tonight?" She giggled.

"No, I've been thinking, though. I . . ." His tongue stuck to the roof of his mouth. He didn't have to hurry. They were alone in Paradise. In more ways than one.

"What? That you love me?" She drew back and touched his face, ran her fingers through his silver hair. "I know that Joseph Clay Carter. I know that. It would take a lot of love to stay in this old house for the past four months. Besides, you tell me every day."

"I do not," he said thickly.

"Yes, you do. You look across the room with those big old baby blue eyes and they tell me. You bring me a mason jar of tea when I'm so deep into a romance book, whether writing, researching, or reading, that I forget about time and that tells me. You scoop the kitty litter without saying a word. Help Rae with her multiplication. Assure Ursula that she will get to wear makeup before she's eighty. That's called standing behind me and it means love," she said.

"I do love you, Mary Jane," he said simply. "I need to say the words every day as well as do the deeds."

"I love you too, Joe Clay," she kissed him lightly on the lips. "It's been four weeks. We've had some fights but we recovered from them. You said for me to trust you. I do. I trust you to come back to me when you go save the world next week. I trust you to keep faithful when you are gone and not even cast a sidewise look at another woman. I don't care if she's rich as Midas," she laughed.

"Mary Jane, will you marry me? I don't have a ring yet, but will you?" He asked.

"Yes, I will. Lord, I was beginning to think I was going to have to ask you," she drew his mouth down for a real kiss.

"Tomorrow? Will you marry me tomorrow morning? The courthouse will be open one more day before the holidays. We could drive to Nocona, stop at the jewelry store and buy a set of rings, go to Montague and get married and I'd have a week with you before I have to leave. We could have Christmas in Paradise as a family," he nuzzled the inside of her neck.

"Okay," she said simply.

"You will. What about the girls?" he asked.

"You trying to get out of a contract again, Joe Clay Carter, like you did at Thanksgiving? When a man asks a woman to marry him and she says yes, it's binding in the courts. Now are you already trying to get out of this? The girls will be ecstatic when they come home and I give them you for Christmas," she told him.

"You really will?" he asked in amazement.

"I really will," she whispered. "But only if you'll take me inside and help me make five batches of Christmas candy, a date nut cake, and . . ."

"What?" he asked.

"Honey, this is going to be the longest night of our lives. We might as well get some work done while we wait for the morning. Tomorrow we'll be standing at the door when they open the jewelry store and I figure the drive to Montague and the marriage will take about an hour. That'll give us a whole afternoon for a honeymoon in Paradise without the girls," she said.

"Mary Jane. Our honeymoon is going to last forever. Trust me," he said.

And she did.